GENTS
A novel

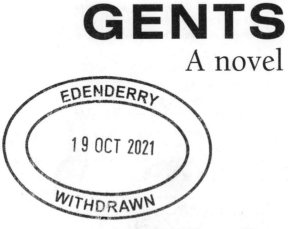

Warwick Collins

FRIDAY
FICTION

First published in Great Britain in 1997 by Marion Boyars Publishers
This paperback edition published in 2007 by Friday Fiction
An imprint of The Friday Project Limited
83 Victoria Street, London SW1H 0HW

www.thefridayproject.co.uk
www.fridaybooks.co.uk

Text © 2007 Warwick Collins

ISBN – 13   978-1-905548-76-7

British Library Cataloguing in Publication Data

A catalogue record for this book is available from the British Library

Cover design by Snowbooks Design
Internal design and typesetting by Maggie Aldred

Printed by MPG Books Ltd

The Publisher's policy is to use paper manufactured from
sustainable sources.

To Scott Pack

CHAPTER 1

At Charing Cross the two underground trains passed each other like tongues of flame. Ez Murphy saw, in the window's reflection between a young girl and an elderly woman, his own face dark with the lights shining white on his broad cheekbones.

The trains roared and razored in the confined tunnel. As they crossed, his faded image, obscure against the glossy dark, was thrown into sudden prominence by the rush of white lights behind it. The faces of the two women became ghostly, obliterated by the surging luminescence.

He was in his early forties, well-dressed, stocky,

broad-shouldered. In the reflection opposite, his hands floated up to adjust his tie, a startling negative against the washed white of his collar. The two trains passed. During the ensuing silence the faces of the women were restored again, two white flowers.

The train traversed several other stations before it finally slid to a stop with a brief squeal of acquiescence. The doors rumbled open. Ez stepped onto the dimly lit platform and walked to the sign marked EXIT. It was eight twenty-two by the station clock. Travelling up the escalator, he put his ticket in the machine, then paused in the concourse. He felt a sudden, inexplicable urge to see daylight. Walking up a flight of grey flagged stairs, he stepped out into the street.

Drifts of London sunlight touched his eyes; a flock of pigeons wheeled above the buildings. Traffic fumes hung over the city.

He approached a sign on a wrought iron stairway which said GENTS. Straightening his tie, he walked down the steps. At the bottom, he faced a turnstile.

He glanced around for assistance, but could see no one. Shrugging his shoulders, he shifted the change in his pocket and put ten pence in the slot. Then he walked through the turnstile and paused to glance around him.

The interior was faced with geometric tiles, white with a motif of green. The floors were meticulously clean. In the background he could hear the occasional hiss of the fountains. On the right of the entrance, set back discreetly into a wall of rough, whitewashed plaster, was a green-painted door marked MANAGER.

Ez adjusted his collar and knocked.

After a while, the door opened. The man facing him was as tall as a beanpole. His clothes hung on his skinny frame. He had that almost albino whiteness of certain Jamaicans on the south side of the island. Standing in the doorway, he considered Ez for a moment.

"Mr Murphy?"

"That's right."

"Josiah Reynolds." He seemed to pause for several seconds, and Ez gained the impression he was trying to work out something. "Come in, come in."

Reynolds stood aside. Ez stepped into a small, neat office with a wooden table and several folding chairs. Against the wall was a filing cabinet, on top of which was a shelf with some grey box files. The only decoration on the walls was a white calendar without pictures, covered by the heavy black print of dates. Ez gained the impression of a pervasive austerity.

Reynolds picked up a clipboard from his desk. He lifted a ball-point from his top pocket.

"Murphy," he read out. "Ezekiel Stanislaus."

Ez nodded.

Reynolds smiled, as though in recognition. He indicated one of the wooden seats.

"Sit down, man."

Reynolds took several paces back and leaned, half seated, on the edge of the table. His long bony wrists emerged from the cuffs. Raising his clipboard, Reynolds consulted his notes.

"You cleaner at Lambeth Council four years. Before that you from Jamaica."

Ez nodded.

"Which part you from?"

"Brixton."

"I mean Jamaica," Reynolds said.

Ez noted the long move of the Adam's apple in Reynolds' bony neck. He tried to guess Reynolds' age. "West Kingston. Greenwich Farm. You know it?"

A thin smile spread across the other man's face. "Course I know it, man," Reynolds said. "Mandy's on George Street. Friday Café. Singular." He shifted a little against the table. "Aunt Mimmy's Place. What was it then? Sideways? What is it now?"

"Cornstocks," Ez said.

"Cornstocks?"

"Selling to Rastas, mostly." Ez paused, then added, "You live there sometime?"

"Once a time."

Ez was delighted. He said, "Bacon juice."

"Bacon juice." Reynolds laughed suddenly. The

corners of his eyes became creased. "All those corner smokers?"

"Still there."

Reynolds smiled. His face shifted back to an expression of watchfulness. "You know what work is here?"

Ez shrugged.

Reynolds said, "Washing out, mopping floors, keeping turnstiles working, maintaining a change box, controlling the kiddies. Keeping order."

"Keeping order?" Ez asked.

"Sometimes. Sometimes things get out of hand in the cubicles."

Ez nodded but he was not certain he had understood.

Reynolds scratched his cheek, a minor gesture of perplexity.

"You religious?" Reynolds asked. "Don' mind my askin'?"

"Adventist, maybe."

Reynolds chuckled. "That makes you."

"You could say."

"How you like Lambeth?" Reynolds asked.

"So-so."

"Strange place, man. Council turnin' itself inside out. Maybe you safer here."

Ez did not answer. In the silence, Reynolds said, "You meet Jason yet?"

"No."

Reynolds nodded and moved to the door. He opened it and called out.

"Jason!"

Reynolds returned and leaned back against the table. He smiled, then seemed content to subside into patois again. "Him no dog – like cat, man. Call, him come in own time."

"He work here?"

"Pass time here," Reynolds said. "Like you and me pass water."

Ez watched the movement of Reynolds' Adam's apple, the swallow before mirth. Reynolds chuckled softly at his joke.

Not long afterwards a figure appeared at the door, of medium height, slender, with wide eyes and Rasta dreadlocks.

Reynolds said, "Jason." He indicated Ez. "Meet him here."

Ez stood up. "Ez Murphy."

Jason seemed to hesitate. Then he moved forward. Seriously, almost carefully, he shook Ez by the hand. Jason's right eye was lazy, the left direct. It took a while to work out which eye was assessing you. Back in Kingston they called it chameleon.

Reynolds turned to address Jason formally. "Look after him. He join us now."

With a brief nod to Reynolds, Jason asked, "You from Kingston?"

"Greenwich."

Jason nodded.

"Loud place."

Reynolds translated, "Loud mean good."

Ez nodded.

"Fat Lion Stevens?" Jason asked.

"He sober."

Jason smiled. "Too bad."

"Better show him the ropes, Jason, man," Reynolds said. "Can't talk all day."

Jason turned and departed. Ez glanced at Reynolds, who nodded once, then turned away towards his desk.

Ez followed Jason into the urinals, into the flowing, bouncing light.

CHAPTER 2

Jason removed a key from his pocket and opened a locker-room door. He handed Ez a green overall.

"Fit you?"

Ez slipped it over his shoulders.

"Seem OK."

Jason reached into the cupboard and brought out an extra mop.

"This for you."

Ez gripped the wooden shaft of the mop. Jason hauled out a big tin bucket with a heavy handle. He handed it to Ez. Jason pointed to a single tap on the wall with a thick enamel basin beneath.

"Main tap there."

Jason indicated some buckets lined neatly against the farther wall of the locker room. Several held plastic containers of green fluid.

"Cleaning. Three teaspoon for a bucket."

"OK."

Jason indicated a row of boxes containing cakes of antiseptic deodorant for the latrines.

"Replacement."

Ez nodded.

"You OK? You got everything?"

Ez smiled. "In the Kingdom."

Ez walked away to the tap, filled the bucket, poured in some cleaning fluid, dipped the mop. He started to work, swinging the mop over the tiled floors.

Jason smiled briefly, put in his earphones, and took up his own mop.

For perhaps half an hour Ez washed the floors with Jason working in the background. He could hear only the faint scratching of Jason's music.

He swung the head of the mop in long sweeps, quartering an area towards the door and Reynolds' office. When he had finished he took a long-handled sponge and began to work back over the wet floors.

There was an uneven flow of customers down the steps, through the rattling turnstiles, to the urinals. He became used to the definitions of space, the silences of the tiles, the occasional footsteps of men as they approached the urinals, paused, then walked back through the turnstiles. After a while the flow of men to and fro from the urinals began to remind him of water in its restless inconstancy.

Ez worked slowly towards the cubicles. They were set out against the farthest wall from the entrance, a line of seventeen in all, with wooden doors and solid mahogany frames. He reached the end of the room, then he turned parallel to the line of cubicles and began to work his way to the adjacent wall.

Behind him, the occasional customer entered a cubicle and bolted the latch. He heard the slam of a door as someone exited from a cubicle and then the sound of metal bearings as he passed through the turnstile.

Later that morning, towards lunch, he stopped, blinked, stretched. A man emerged from a nearby cubicle. Ez gained an impression of a City suit, of early middle age, of the brief shine of baldness beneath thinning hair. The man passed through the turnstiles and began to walk up the stairs beyond. He seemed to drift upwards, as though in a trance, towards the grey light of the exit.

Ez put down the mop and walked over to the cubicle.

He opened the door to visit the cubicle himself. But before he could enter, a second man came out, brushing past him, not catching his eye.

In his initial incomprehension it seemed to Ez curiously like a magical trick – two rabbits from the same hat. Or perhaps *déjà vu*. He tried to assemble an impression of the second man, of a white face with fair hair and almost albino eyelids, of a grey City suit like the first, and an air of calmness or preoccupation. He was younger and fairer than the first man, though they might have come from the same firm, the same office. Ez watched him walk through the turnstiles and up the steps. He listened to the final faint patter of his leather-soled shoes as he disappeared from view into clouded daylight.

He glanced at Jason, who was standing a few yards away, leaning on his mop, watching Ez equivocally. Jason smiled, shook his head, and turned away. He began to mop the floor again. Ez heard the furred music from his headphones, like an insect fluttering against a pane.

CHAPTER 3

Later that afternoon the three of them, Ez, Reynolds, and Jason, were taking tea in Reynolds' office.

Reynolds said, "How your first day going?"

"OK, man."

Jason sat in his chair chewing a biscuit.

Ez said, "Funny thing happen to me."

Reynolds sipped his tea. "What?"

"I was wanting to visit a cubicle – you know. Someone come out and so I know it is free. I go to open the door and ... another man come out."

Reynolds watched him carefully, as though trying to calculate Ez's comprehension.

After a while, Reynolds said, "So?"

Ez shrugged. "I don't understand it. Two men in there."

Reynolds sipped his tea and chewed his biscuit.

"What don't you understand?"

"One man sitting, one man waiting. Why don't he wait outside?"

Ez looked at Reynolds' face. Some faint appreciation entered his thoughts.

Reynolds considered him. He observed several expressions move across Ez's features.

Ez said, "You don't –"

Jason seemed embarrassed more by Ez's innocence than the subject under discussion. He shook his head and looked away.

Finally Reynolds said, "You don't know?"

"Don't know what?"

"Happening all the time," Jason said.

"What happening?" Ez asked.

"All the time," Reynolds repeated. "Reptiles."

Ez looked from one face to the other.

"Men are ...? Two in ..."

"Sometimes three."

"No."

Jason said, "One time, five."

"Five?" Ez was incredulous.

Jason nodded. "Five walk out."

They paused. Ez sipped his tea and considered. Neither of the other two spoke.

After a few moments, Ez said, "What you do about it?"

Reynolds shrugged. "Stop it getting out of hand."

Jason moved on his chair and nodded. "That the truth."

Ez said, "Why they wanting to do this, man?"

"We don't ask why, man," Reynolds said. His voice had the singsong of patois. "We don't keep their conscience, we only keeping order."

"Why they do it here?" Ez asked. "Why not somewhere else?"

"Where else?"

"Better than out on the street," Jason said.

Reynolds and Jason laughed softly. Jason said, as if by way of confirmation, "Better than the pavement."

Ez waited patiently for their mirth to subside.

"They got a compulsion," Reynolds explained. "You see them, looking about, hoping to catch someone's eye."

"What you do to stop them?"

"We can't stop them looking about, man. If they loiter too long, maybe, we ask them to move along."

"Sometimes another one come," Jason said. "They go into a cubicle. Two of them."

"How?"

"When you not looking. One go first. Wait awhile. Then another. Slippery, man. But once you know they in there, you can make it difficult. You knock on the door. If nothing happen, you put a big stick under the door, rattle it about."

"A big stick?"

Reynolds stood up, walked to the farthest corner, and picked up an oversize wooden walking-stick that leaned against the wall.

"You knock this against their ankles."

Jason said, "You rattle their cage, man." He laughed openly, shaking his head.

"Sometimes it doesn't work," Reynolds said. "Sometimes nothing happen."

Ez swallowed. "What then?"

"You just have to wait for them to come out."

Ez didn't bother to hide his consternation. He knew he was under observation but he had moved beyond surprise. He looked from one to the other. Reynolds gave him a straight stare. Jason softly shook his head and turned away.

In the evening, as Ez took off his overalls and put his mop in the cupboard, Reynolds asked, "First day all right?"

"Fine."

"Think you last?"

"Believe so."

Jason drifted out on his way out through the side-door.

"Bye, man."

Reynolds put on a scarf and coat. "See you tomorrow."

Ez nodded. He followed Reynolds out into the winter dusk. He heard Reynolds lock the heavy door behind them, using several keys. Then he walked towards the underground station, past the grey and blue fluorescent lighting of the shops.

CHAPTER 4

Martha set a meal of mackerel and maize on the table in front of Ez. She sat down and watched him eat, her elbows on the table, her chin resting on her hands.

Ez took several mouthfuls. He said, "You not eatin'?"

"I ate earlier."

Ez nodded. He glanced up at Martha and saw she was still watching him.

Martha said, "So how was it?"

"OK."

"You like the others?"

"Mr Reynolds is the supervisor. Jason is the other cleaner."

Martha said, "You get on?"

Between mouthfuls, Ez replied, "I get on fine." He paused. "Where's Stevie?"

"He's out."

"Not with that bad crowd?"

"Maybe not," Martha said. "He tell me different."

"Some fellows from West Kingston living round Buckle Street. Northampton estate. Some real bad boys. Seen them on the streets. Easy money." He moved mackerel onto his fork with his knife. "Maybe afterwards, I go take a look for Stevie."

Martha put a restraining hand on his elbow.

Ez watched her hand, the pale fingernails. He always liked the way the flesh sat on her fingers, firm.

Martha said, "I know where he is."

"Where?"

"At the hairdresser's." She paused. "Biziou's."

"Getting a haircut?"

Martha smiled. "No. Learnin'."

"Learnin'?"

"Learnin'. Takin' up a new job, like you."

Ez's fork hovered.

"Stevie?"

Martha nodded. "It's a good trade."

Ez said, "He don't play football no more."

"Ez." Martha's fingers seemed to caress his arm. "Steve's good at football, but he's not so good. It's not an easy life."

"Application," Ez said. He watched her hand retreat, almost with regret, then he returned to his eating. Martha seemed about to leave the table. He felt conciliatory.

"He's good," Ez said. "He could be something. The best in his youth club. Nothing to stop him. One day maybe he play for a club, maybe Arsenal."

"Ez, don't make Stevie do what you didn't do."

"He's different," Ez said. "I had a wife and kid, responsibilities. He got none. He could still do it."

"Training, day in day out, for his father's ambition."

When he had finished, Martha said, "You want some more?"

Ez shook his head.

"I go make some coffee."

Ez watched as she got up and went to the cooker. He glanced down at the table in thought. After a while, he pushed his plate away from him. He had wanted to say something about the work, about his consternation and doubt.

"How your day?" he called out. She worked part time at the social services department at Lambeth, doing clerical work. The extra income was useful.

"Not so bad."

He could see Martha's back through the kitchen door as she rinsed plates while waiting for the kettle to boil. By the poise of her neck and the angle of her head he could tell that she was thinking about something. She was not usually so uncommunicative. He knew that the subject of Stevie affected her too.

CHAPTER 5

Ez hung up his coat and hat. He put on his green overall. At the end of the room Reynolds was talking to Jason, outlining an object with his hands. Jason nodded in greeting to Ez over Reynolds' shoulder.

Occasional customers moved back and forth from the urinals. Sometimes the door of a cubicle banged.

Ez picked up a pail with a small bristly brush and some cakes of disinfectant. In another bucket he had placed a pair of large tongs.

Approaching the urinals, Ez stopped at each one. Using the tongs, he lifted the old urine-streaked cakes of disinfectant and dropped them carefully into one of the buckets. Then he scrubbed the urinal with the bristly brush. When he had finished, he picked up a new cake of disinfectant and placed it in each urinal.

A tall, stooped man puffed softly with the effort of carrying a large shopping bag. He was standing crouched over himself like a question mark. Ez had to move around him.

Ez repeated the process on the next urinal. Removing the old cake of disinfectant, he began to scrub the enamel walls.

The man said cheerily, "New here?"

Ez finished scrubbing and reached for a cake of disinfectant. "Not long."

The man said, pleasantly enough, "Always something new to learn, isn't there?"

Ez nodded.

The man coughed, shifted in his space. He zipped himself up, then reached for the heavy paper bag.

Ez watched him walk through the turnstile. He went back to work.

❋

During the break, Reynolds said to Ez, "You have a family?"

The three of them, Ez, Reynolds, and Jason, were seated at the table. Steam rose from their tea.

"A wife and kid," Ez said.

"How old your kid?"

Ez blew across the surface of the tea. "Seventeen."

Reynolds nodded. He sipped his tea, put it down, added another spoonful of sugar, then raised it and sipped again.

Reynolds said, "I got two."

"That so?"

"Grown up now."

Ez nodded.

Reynolds indicated Jason with his head.

Reynolds winked at Ez. Jason was leaning forward, his elbows resting on his knees. He seemed locked in his own thoughts.

Ez said to Jason, "Jason? Married too?"

Jason was quiet. Reynolds interceded. "Jason got two."

"Two children?"

"Two wives," Reynolds commented. He chuckled. Ez glanced toward Jason. Jason seemed as taciturn as ever, sipping his tea.

Reynolds said, "He leave one wife in Kingston. He come here. He marry another. Wife from Kingston also come. That why he turn Rasta."

"Rasta?"

"Rasta can take more than one woman."

Reynolds appeared mightily amused at this legerdemain. He joshed Jason affectionately.

"Ol' Jason," Reynolds said. "He flow where de wind flow."

Jason gave a bemused smile.

In the silence, Ez sipped his tea.

✳

Later that afternoon, Ez was washing down a lower part of one tiled wall adjacent to the urinals. He was down on one knee. Around him men walked past. As he cleaned he observed their ankles and shoes go past him. After a while he raised himself on both his knees and pressed his back with the palms of his hands against the nagging pain that occasionally affected his lower trunk. Slowly he moved his shoulders from side to side.

He started to work again, kneeling on a small rubber mat, using the scrubbing brush on the floor tiles closest the wall.

He was at a place where he could see under the wooden side screens of the cubicles. A door slammed softly, and a pair of shoes appeared in the nearest cubicle. Ez went back to his scrubbing. Doors opened and closed as individuals came and went.

When Ez looked again there were two pairs of shoes in the nearest cubicle, facing each another. As he watched, one pair of shoes turned the other way.

Ez glanced around him. He could see Jason at the farthest end of the room. Reynolds was in his office.

Ez stood up. He walked to the end of the room, where Jason was washing the floor, taking long, even sweeps with the mop. Against the background noise of the urinals – water flushing, the occasional door banging – Ez could hear the echo in his temples.

He tapped Jason's shoulder. Jason withdrew the earplugs from his ears.

"What matter?"

He said to Jason, "Two in de nearest cubicle."

Jason nodded, as if he had been told the time of day. He removed his gloves and set them down on the sink. He stepped towards Reynolds' office and knocked softly on the door. He waited for Reynolds' call and entered, closing the door behind him.

Ez glanced at the cubicle. It seemed, in the fervent silence, that it was vibrating slightly, like a washing machine, as though various pieces of clothing were being thrown against the side. Then the machine seemed to switch itself off, to utter a soft sigh.

Ez glanced in the direction of Reynolds' office. He tried to make out the faint sounds of Jason and Reynolds in discussion.

A few seconds later Jason emerged carrying the heavy walking-stick. Ez followed him.

Holding the stick in his left hand, Jason struck the side of the cubicle with the flat of his right palm, two big slow hits. He waited a few seconds in the silence that gathered around him. He thumped once again. Silence thickened around the cubicle.

After a few moments Jason handed Ez the walking-stick.

Jason knelt down, lined his eye along the floor, and raised a hand for the stick. Ez passed it to him. Jason observed the position of the ankles inside the cubicles. Taking careful aim, he thrust the stick under the partition.

Ez watched him, bracing himself with one arm, kneeling on the floor tiles, sighting the stick like a rifleman, swinging it back and forth against the ankles inside.

"Come on," Jason said. He was speaking softly, almost to himself. "Come on ouda dere."

After a few moments Jason stood up and gestured to Ez to stand back. The door swung open. A man rushed out and headed for the turnstiles, leaning forward as though against a wind. Ez was aware of a hefty body like a barrel, of hair slicked back, of an almost animal-like power as the man snapped down the turnstile bar and then took the outer stairs two at a time upwards into the sallow light.

Jason winked at Ez.

Without warning, a second man followed, thinner than the first, his hands in the pockets of his leather jacket, walking briskly through the turnstiles. He left behind the expensive odour of cologne. Ez turned back to Jason.

"Givin' de reptile de escape route, man," Jason said. "Dem go like frightened eel."

Ez was too surprised to comment. He merely nodded.

Afterwards, when the three of them were eating their sandwich lunches, Reynolds, in between mouthfuls, addressed Jason.

"You use the stick today, man?"

"Rattle one cage. Two reptile out, swimmin' downstream."

Out of curiosity, Ez said, "Why you callin' dem reptiles?"

Reynolds ate and considered. "They cold, man. Don't speak. One on one. You can't get them off, like a dog with a bone." He paused, sipping his tea. "Ask Jason. He expert."

Jason smiled to himself and continued to eat. After a while Jason said, "All aroun' here, men in office, speakin' on telephone, telling secretary, firin', hirin', doin' accounts, makin' money, man. Put down telephone, walk out sometime, come in here." He indicated the direction of the cubicles with a gesture of his head. "Meet another one in there."

Jason paused after his homily. He took a bite, then added cheerfully, "All time, man. Every day."

Ez looked at him, shook his head, and concentrated on eating his own sandwich. The other two ate as though famished. Martha had given Ez banana and pilchards, his favourite filling. It struck him then how odd was this blend of domestic arrangements with the subject matter in hand.

"You learnin', man," Reynolds said quietly. "You learnin'."

CHAPTER 6

In the course of the following weeks Ez began to
appreciate the quality of silence. In between the
slamming of doors, the pressed hush, it was as if the
silence was a living force, was scratching against the
walls.

He began to understand the grammar of the
place, the movement of footsteps, the declension of
doors, the patterns of approach to the urinals and the
cubicles.

Some of the men seemed to drift down the stairs
in a somnambulistic trance. Most of them had a
single purpose – to relieve themselves – and then

return to the day. In the chamber beneath the earth time itself seemed suspended. No one made eye contact because it could be misinterpreted. Ez learned never to look a customer in the eye unless he was directly addressed.

He became aware of the space around a person, and of the squares of space in which individuals moved. Each man's grid seemed to move with him. Sometimes a particular man might hold his attention like a singer in a spotlight, but it was an indirect surveillance, by means of the senses of hearing and smell and vibration. Ez could hear the sound of a man's footsteps across the floor, the creak of his clothes. He would listen for the speed and hesitancy of footfall, the faint squeal of rubber soles, the flatness of leather, the heel touching before the toe, the creak and slam of a cubicle door.

He became aware of each new customer as a brief flare of presence, a ghost at the perimeter of the eye, and could tell from the sound of a person's footsteps whether he was in one part of the room or another.

Close to the shiny urinal walls the sounds were precise and sharp. In a corner they seemed hollower. Adjacent the rough concrete outside Reynolds' office they were absorbed and deadened.

He became an expert in tracking disembodied sounds, as sensitive as any animal. It was possible to tell from the sound alone which cubicle had opened or closed. The doors of the seventeen cubicles were like a musical scale. Each hollow space they enclosed had a different frequency. The flushing of the cistern in cubicle three had a different sound from cubicle eleven. Sometimes he could tell the mass or weight of the individual occupying a cubicle by the shape of slight sounds within enclosed space, the click of a belt buckle, the slide of trousers, the sigh of peace.

It was not just a heightening of the senses – in the same way, it was said, that the other senses of the blind became sharply attuned – but an enhanced recognition of pattern. The visitors were pallid ghosts that moved in the mind.

Beneath the smell of urine or faeces, of chlorine

in the water, the disinfectants and floor polishes, the rinses and scourers, there was the faint scent of the others who shared their domain, the smell of fear and repression. Reynolds, Jason and he were the denizens of a separate republic. Amongst themselves, their patois became more pronounced. More than a means of communication between them, it was a bond that excluded others. Through emphasis, they could shift the edge of meaning away from the understanding of others.

Time seemed to stand still. The three of them moved between opening and closing time in a curiously self-enclosed space.

It was only when he went home to Martha that Ez was struck by time itself, the sudden, unexpected flower of physical existence. He was assailed by the smells of cooking, the bloom of Martha's skin. It seemed his entire world opened to a different dimension.

CHAPTER 7

One evening, Martha said, "You know what I see today?"

Ez and Martha were seated at table. They had finished their meal.

"What?"

"Moulson, the butchers. Importing special Jamaican delicacies. Tell me they got demand in the local population."

"What they got?" Ez asked.

"Goat meat. Fat wood-dove. Sassafreet lizards. You like fried lizard?"

Ez shook his head. He rubbed his stomach.

"I'm off de reptiles."

A look of concern passed across Martha's face.

"Poor man," Martha said. "Your indigestion?"

"Antacid, man."

Martha said, "I'll get you some pills maybe."

CHAPTER 8

The man wore long hair in a pony-tail. His face was that strange, pasty white that seemed curiously incomplete. Ez sensed something like need leaching out of him.

"Work here?" he asked.

Ez nodded.

The man was standing at the urinals. He looked around, across the ceiling. His profile seemed as sharp as an axe blade. "Not much of a place, is it?"

Ez shrugged.

"Not much of a place to work, I mean," the man said.

Ez set out the rubber mat on the floor and knelt on it, then began to scrub the tiles, working back and forth methodically.

"It's disgusting," the man said, almost to himself. Then he added, as though it were a detail, "disgusting what they do in places like this."

Ez tried to work out the line of his interest. The man continued to look around as though he were considering buying the place. He had a strange voice, as if the sound was scratched.

"Know what I would do?"

Ez didn't answer. He guessed that the man was uninterested in what he said.

"Cut off their fucking bollocks," the man said. "Stuff them in their mouths."

Ez paused, then continued with his scrubbing.

The man said, "You can hear that, can't you?"

In the background Ez heard the first and then the second thump of a cubicle door. His mind was alerted by odd conjunctions, the way that two minuses sometimes make a plus. He listened to the silence in the interior of the cubicle, the sense of heaviness in the atmosphere.

The man had finished urinating and now he zipped himself up. He too was listening.

Ez turned his attention to the cubicle again. It seemed to him that he could hear tight, strange little drubbing sounds, like someone struggling out of a coffin; the mind was both repelled and pulled towards the sound.

The man heard it too. He lowered his voice to a whisper. "You going to do something, then?"

Ez continued to scrub the floor. He waited for the man to leave. He intended to alert Reynolds and Jason, but he was determined that the man should not be involved in what might happen next.

Something in the man's voice changed. He seemed to be carrying some indefinable weight. Without warning, the man said calmly, "You shagging, shagging cunt."

Slowly, Ez swung the brush to and fro. There seemed to be no answer he could give. The man was responding instead to some internal pressure that Ez could only guess at.

"You could stop those shagging bastards in there. If you wanted."

Ez felt his mouth go dry. He continued to scrub the floor, as though he had not heard.

The man reached into his pocket and withdrew something with a single, smooth gesture. Ez heard the faint click, and felt the coldness of a blade on the back of his neck.

"Yes, you," the man said.

Ez stopped scrubbing. He could not find words to speak. The man and he were both listening to the sounds of the cubicle, as though they were complicit. Around them, the silence seemed to hang like mist. Ez tried to remember where Jason had gone. He had been mopping the floor; now he seemed to have dissolved from his position at the other end of the room.

"You're as bad as they are," the man whispered. "Worse."

In the background, Ez heard the faint sound of a door being closed quietly and then the barely discernible pad of footsteps. Out of the corner of his eye he saw Reynolds' shoes approaching and, behind them, Jason's trainers.

Reynolds was standing beside the man, a tall column of air. For several seconds the man was silent, leaning over Ez, his knife laid carefully on the back of Ez's neck.

"Best you go," Reynolds suggested.

The man stood still for several seconds. Ez had the impression he seemed to be searching in his mind for Reynolds' presence, exploring its contours. It was as if he became aware of Reynolds only by degrees.

The man said calmly, as though calculating a response, "You another fucking nigger?"

Still Reynolds did not move. Ez looked for some faint shift in Reynolds' stance.

"Best you go now," Reynolds suggested again.

Ez felt the blade of the knife turn backward and forward slowly, as if the man were considering whether to sever the muscles on Ez's neck.

Without warning, the man casually nodded, as though affirming something to himself. Folding his knife, he moved calmly towards the turnstiles. He seized the steel bar and swung on it. Then he ascended the stairs two by two into the waiting light.

"How you?" Reynolds asked, after a brief interval of silence.

Ez stood up, breathing softly. His bowels seemed to be made of water. "OK, I think."

"Good thing Jason see you," Reynolds said affably. "Come tell me."

Beside him Jason said nothing, only smiled.

Ez walked to one of the cubicles and closed the door. He dropped his trousers. What flowed out of him seemed to be the sum of his dark fears. He sat on the seat and thought about the man, about his paleness, about the way his fingers gripped the knife, how the blade lay casually on his neck as though the man were considering opening an oyster. He expelled his terrors into the pan.

Afterwards, Reynolds said, "Fear, man, de finest laxative. Clean out de system."

Ez said, "How you know he no come back, bring knife again?"

"Don' know," Reynolds said. He shrugged. "No fey be fearsome. One day coming to me what come to us all."

"Maybe," Ez said.

"You learn sometime," Reynolds said kindly. "Reptile not dangerous. Danger come from man who hate reptile. Maybe we best be doing sometin' about dis place."

CHAPTER 9

In the Gents the following day, Ez was cleaning the floor, moving across the green tiles towards the cubicles. He watched the grey slick of water fan out briefly from the tail of the mop, then fade as the thin film dried.

Reynolds and Jason were in close discussion at the other end of the room. They had taken up odd positions. Reynolds was casually turned away, leaning with both hands over a hand basin. Jason was standing sideways to him. Both men spoke briefly and cryptically. Ez knew from something indefinable about their attitudes that they were discussing a subject of particular importance. From time to time, Jason glanced casually over his shoulder at a mirror about half-way down the room.

It took Ez a few seconds to understand that the object of this casual surveillance was a man standing at the other end of the room, framed in the mirror's reflection.

Ez continued to mop the floor in long sweeps. He glanced at the man, who wore smart denims and trainer shoes. There was something neat and circumspect about him. He was washing his hands slowly and calmly, but his attention was directed firmly into a mirror above the wash-basin. He stared into it intently, as if into a room or into the depths of water.

Ez noticed that Reynolds and Jason were speaking softly, in patois. Closer to them than the man, Ez could just make out their voices above the occasional hiss of the water fountains.

"What doing now?" Reynolds asked.

"Standing, man," Jason said. "Floating."

"Which one he look at?"

"Cubicle eight."

"Seen him before?"

Jason nodded. "Sometime."

"What doing now?"

"Rubbernecking. Want to join de two in number eight."

"You reckon two?"

"Reckon."

Jason paused, seemed to consider. "Got big compulsion. Going green under de gills."

Reynolds glanced up at the ceiling. His jaw hardened as he seemed to come to a decision. Ez saw the movement of light along his jawbone, where the muscle tightened.

It was Reynolds who initiated the action. Something inside him seemed to pause, gather itself, then uncoil. He turned and started to move briskly down the long room. Jason swung in with him, partly behind and to his side.

Ez glanced back at the man, who seemed

oblivious of the suddenly changed circumstances, the altered configuration of forces. Reynolds and Jason advanced down the room, side by side. Ez watched them go by.

The man had been concentrating in the mirror. Now at last he saw Reynolds and Jason approaching. His concentration seemed to snap. He darted across to the door to cubicle number eight and gave three raps. Then he pivoted towards the turnstiles and was about to make off.

Jason caught up with him before the barrier and gave him a strong shove. The man stumbled and fell.

At that moment it seemed to Ez that the room was filled not only with movement but with a confusion of noise, as though loudspeakers had been turned on. Reynolds was shouting, "Get out of here!"

Beside him, Jason called, "Seen you before!"

With surprising swiftness, the man gathered himself, rising to his feet with a curious grace. He attempted to move off again, as though he had stumbled and fallen accidentally. Without looking directly at his two persecutors, he held up a calm hand and swerved towards the gates. Ez watched the man pass through the turnstiles as if he were swimming through a current.

Reynolds had positioned himself outside the door of cubicle eight.

A second man, tall and thin, walked out briskly. Reynolds tapped his heel with his own shoe and drove his shoulder hard against him, tripping him up. The man fell over heavily on the tiles and writhed there silently, like a beetle upturned. At the same time, Jason wrenched open the door of the cubicle. Reaching in, he hauled out a youth in a T-shirt, who blinked in the sudden light.

It seemed to Ez as if Reynolds and Jason were deliberately offending the calm, that they were making their outrage felt to all the other occupants of the cubicles. Reynolds shouted, "We call the police!" Beside him, Jason was yelling, "We got your identity!"

As the man and the youth scrambled out,

Reynolds called out after them, "I write to your families!"

The sentence echoed through the empty turnstiles. Once through, the older man straightened his tie and walked up the stairs with an attempt at dignity. Behind him, the youth turned back and shuffled and jogged impatiently at the base of the stairs. Out of defiance, perhaps, he remained within sight beyond the turnstiles. Jason moved towards him. Affecting not to notice Jason's approach, the youth turned and ran jauntily up the steps, as though he had remembered an appointment. His white trainers with their black soles ascended the stairs two at a time into the waiting light – white, black, white, black.

CHAPTER 10

Reynolds and Jason turned towards each another. Ez noticed that neither met the other's eyes directly. Jason appeared drawn into his own thoughts.

"Tea-time," Reynolds announced.

Ez looked through the empty turnstiles. The Gents seemed to have gone cold, as though traumatised by the sudden eruption of violence.

Reynolds, seeing Ez hesitate, said, "Come on, man. Let de place calm down."

Inside the office, light descended from the skylight. The kettle shrieked and shook as it came to the boil. Jason clicked the switch and filled the pot.

Outside, they heard the door of one of the cubicles slam. Jason said, "Other ones clearing out now."

A second door slammed. In the silence that followed, Jason put sugar and milk on the tray and carried it across to Reynolds' desk. He set out cups and saucers on the table.

Reynolds formally poured three cups. He handed one to Jason and the other to Ez.

Ez had recovered from the rapid beating of his heart and the dryness of his throat. He said, "You pretty rough, you two."

Reynolds tipped two spoons of sugar into his tea and began to stir. For several seconds no one spoke. Jason pulled up another chair and poured milk into his tea.

Ez said, "Rougher than maybe you need."

Reynolds took several sips of the hot tea. He seemed unconcerned. "We keep getting instructions from de council to stop them, man. Carrying out orders."

"Why today?" Ez asked.

"Yesterday you get threatened with knife," Reynolds replied.

"Not by a reptile."

"Same thing, man," Reynolds said. "Same solution. We clean out de reptiles. No more provocation."

Jason said, "They learn a lesson pretty quick. Teach one, teach all."

Ez paused to consider. Reynolds seemed relaxed. Jason appeared his usual nonchalant self.

"Maybe," Ez said, "they wait outside afterward, maybe attack you."

Reynolds finished stirring his tea. He put down the spoon, then blew across the surface. "Maybe they want their faces known too, man. Maybe they want identify themselves to the police? They lucky we don't get them arrested."

Jason nodded.

"This place get a bad reputation," Reynolds continued. "Three years ago, the police put in a surveillance team, hide in one cubicle, spy on another. That what we get again if we don't act up rough sometime."

Outside, the Gents seemed to have settled. Ez could hear the faint footsteps of an occasional customer traversing the tiles to the urinals. He had been surprised by the sudden emptying of the cubicles after the fracas, as if an entire local population had abandoned its ecological niche in panic.

He tried to remember how many of the cubicle doors were closed, how many were occupied. He guessed that almost every single one was occupied at the time Reynolds had initiated the offensive. It occurred to Ez for the second time that day that Reynolds and Jason were playing to this audience, to the aggregation of silent men behind the cubicle doors.

"Scare 'em good," Jason said, then added, "Better for us. Better for them."

Ez nodded, more out of the habit of agreement than out of enthusiasm.

CHAPTER 11

It had been Martha's wish to have furniture made of the local Jamaican woods – cedar, mahoe, bullet wood, break-axe, Spanish elm, and ebony. She and Ez had a vase made of the dark, heavy wood of the lignum vitae, the national flower. The wood was so heavy it would sink in water.

Martha had shipped from Mandeville large cedar cupboards that had belonged to her father. Ez loved the cedar for its scent, for its perfumed sense of well-being. The grain of the wood was a light red that was more fiery and full of life than mahogany.

Martha lay turned away from him. He knew from

the sound of her breathing that she was awake. After a while Martha said, "What you thinking about?"

"Whitey."

Martha shifted onto her back and faced the ceiling. It seemed to Ez they were floating in the darkness together, bound by their thoughts.

"What about Whitey?"

"Whitey wake up in de morning, eat his breakfast, kiss his wife goodbye, pat his chillen on de head. Then he go to the Gents, get in a cubicle with another man, drop his trousers."

Around him the darkness seemed to turn over, to fold in on itself.

Martha said, "What?" She was half amused. "With another man?"

Ez said, "I watch their feet under the cubicle. Sometime their feet pointin' the same way. Sometime one man kneel in front of another. Sometime other things."

Martha paused. "You joking?"

"I'm not joking," Ez said. "Happens all the time."

He could sense her turning her thoughts this way and that in the dark.

"What you do about it?"

"Mr Reynolds and Jason, they have a war. Keepin' back the tide of perversion. Always looking to throw someone out."

"You help them?"

"Sometime."

Martha was silent for several seconds. She said softly, "You not liking your work?"

"Strange thing is, after a while you don't notice it. Just one of the facts."

Martha turned towards him. He felt the equable shake of the bed and the movement of her large hips. He moved to her, into her warmth.

Her perplexed face studied him for a few seconds. She relaxed. "Everyone different," Martha said. "Some people different shakes. Some people gay."

Ez was disinclined to argue. He felt himself sinking downwards into darkness, into silence, towards Jamaica. But something niggled him, some imp of accuracy. He heard his own voice as though at a distance.

"Maybe these people not gay. Gay men mostly don't have to come to dis place. Go to other places. Dese men family men, lonely men."

"Family?"

"Mr Reynolds tell me about one. See him going into office. Solicitor, lawyer, something. He see same man with family, driving wife and chillen."

Martha closed her eyes in concentration, then opened them again.

"Strange world."

Ez watched the light bloom on her cheekbones, the faint gloss on her eyelids. Her eyes were still half open, though it was too dark to see her expression.

❇

At lunchtime the following day, Ez, Reynolds and Jason were eating their sandwiches.

Reynolds said, "Tell you something." He chewed his sandwich and then spoke again. "What is most fearsome to reptiles?"

"What is?" Ez asked.

Reynolds pointed to a camera hanging by its strap on the wall.

"Identification."

"You take photographs?"

Reynolds shook his head. "Just threaten."

"You don't photograph?"

"Don't even put film in de camera."

"Why not?"

"Dangerous, man. If reptile think you got his photograph, maybe he desperate, try to take the camera. I just wave it, maybe I raise it, get a sight of him in de lens." He took another bite from the sandwich. "Psychology."

The three of them ate their food in silence.

Jason said, "You know what?" He moved his jaws while he considered. "Dis morning I see two men go into number three. Fetch walking-stick. Get down on de floor, rap de ankles. No one move. Hit de ankles again. Nothing happen."

Reynolds said amiably, "Reptile."

Jason chewed reflectively. "I'm getting nowhere. So now I'm putting my head under de door, I'm looking up, I'm seeing dese white cheeks."

"Go wan, man."

"I'm looking up, I'm lining de walking-stick up between de cheeks. I'm getting de aim. Pushing upward."

Jason made a graphic upward gesture with his free hand.

Reynolds said, "You terrible liar, Jason." After a while he asked, "What happen?"

Jason gave an imitative high-pitched giggle of pleasure.

Reynolds snorted with laughter. "You very worst liar, know dat?"

"No liar," Jason said.

Reynolds said, with undisguised admiration, "Biggest liar I ever met."

"I'm telling de truth."

"How for me?"

"De truth."

"How for me tell?"

"Sniff de stick."

Reynolds shook with laughter.

"I no sniff de stick, man. You best liar." Addressing Ez, he said, "You want to sniff de stick?"

"I'm eating lunch, man."

The three of them laughed quietly. Reynolds changed the subject.

"Mrs Steerhouse coming today."

"Steerhouse?" Ez asked.

"Inspector from council. Routine visit. She friendly. Come every month."

They finished their sandwiches and swept the crumbs from the table.

Later, when Ez was cleaning out the lavatories, scrubbing the bowls with a stiff brush and flushing the cisterns, he emerged from one of the cubicles and saw a woman in her early forties, blonde and cheerful, waving to attract his attention at the turnstiles.

He put down his mop and bucket, then walked over to the turnstiles and pressed a button to disengage the mechanism. He stood aside to allow Mrs Steerhouse to move her ample hips through.

"Thank you," Mrs Steerhouse said.

Ez nodded. He stepped forward and knocked on Reynolds' door. The door opened. Reynolds was standing there, tall as a rake.

"Mrs Steerhouse," Reynolds said. "Come in."

"Afternoon, Mr Reynolds."

The door closed.

Ez continued to move from one lavatory to another, cleaning out the bowls.

Perhaps twenty minutes later the manager's door opened again. Reynolds' head and torso leaned out. He called, "Ez, come in, man."

Inside Reynolds' office, Mrs Steerhouse and Jason were seated at the table, both with cups of tea.

Standing up like a formal host, Reynolds

introduced Ez. "Mrs Steerhouse, Ezekiel Murphy."

Ez leaned across the table and shook hands with Mrs Steerhouse, who gave a cheerful smile.

"Mr Murphy."

Reynolds handed Ez his cup of tea.

"Thank you," Ez said.

Reynolds pulled up an extra chair, indicated Ez should sit down, and followed suit himself.

"Mrs Steerhouse saying we got a problem."

Ez turned towards her. She had china-blue eyes, an almost relentlessly cheerful expression. There was a watchfulness which lay beneath her geniality. She said, "I'll repeat what I've just said. There's been an instruction from the Social Services Committee. There have been more complaints that this particular Gents is an habitual place of assignation."

Ez paused on the unfamiliar phrases. Reynolds translated. "Too many reptile."

Ez nodded cautiously and again turned his attention to her.

Mrs Steerhouse said, "We've had complaints for

several years. The activity is sometimes called 'cottaging'."

She cleared her throat.

Ez said, "Cottaging?"

"It's nothing to do with the present management. I'm afraid this establishment has always had that reputation, ever since I can remember. What's happened recently is that the council has become more sensitive to the occasional complaints from normal – that is to say, *bona fide* – users. One or two of the customers have been propositioned. One elderly gentleman said he witnessed an act he'd rather not witness again."

Reynolds nodded. "Terrible ting."

"As you know, a public convenience is defined in law as a public place. Therefore any sexual acts between men on these premises are unlawful."

"We understand, Mrs Steerhouse."

"In view of the circumstances, I've been asked to conduct an investigation and make a report."

The silence seemed to move between them.

Reynolds said, "What happen if the report ...?"

"Is negative?" Mrs Steerhouse asked. Her answer came back so briskly it seemed almost as though she had rehearsed it. "The council may decide to take action – action which might include closing down the establishment."

The word "establishment" seemed to amuse Jason. He said softly to himself, "Establishment, man," until Reynolds quietened him with a stare.

"As things stand, then," Mrs Steerhouse continued, "I'm here to issue a formal warning. If, during the next three months, there is no decrease in the reported activities, the chances are that the premises will be shut down. That means, I'm afraid, that you will lose your jobs."

It seemed to Ez that the silence drifted between them like light. After a few moments Reynolds said, "We do everything we can to keep order. You expecting us to clean de place up entirely?"

"What precisely do you mean?" Mrs Steerhouse asked.

"I mean," Reynolds said, "you want us to accompany each person into de cubicles? How else we make sure nuttin' happen?"

Mrs Steerhouse seemed flustered. Two traces of pink appeared in her cheeks. "There will always be occasional incidents in a busy metropolitan latrine, Mr Reynolds, but I am sure we all agree that in the meantime the reputation of this place must improve."

Ez was aware of the illumination from the skylight beating down on the table.

Reynolds said, "We understand."

"Good." Mrs Steerhouse smiled pleasantly. She put down her cup. "Excellent tea, if I may say so."

She rose to her feet.

"Well, I think I must be leaving." To Reynolds and Jason, she said, "Good to see you both again." To Ez she said, "Hope you settle in your new job."

Ez nodded. Mrs Steerhouse picked up her handbag. As she was about to leave the door Jason said, "Mrs Steerhouse."

Mrs Steerhouse turned back.

"Yes, Jason?"

Jason produced the walking-stick from behind his back.

"We were discussin' dis stick. Dere is an odd smell on de end, puzzlin' us."

"A smell," Mrs Steerhouse said. "Really?"

Jason proffered up the end of the walking-stick to Mrs Steerhouse's nostrils.

"Don' rightly know what it remindin' me of."

Sniffing the stick, for a brief moment Mrs Steerhouse's eyes met Jason's.

"It's a bit ripe, whatever it is," Mrs Steerhouse said.

She smiled, withdrew her nose from the stick, opened the door, and said cheerfully, "Goodbye, everyone."

The three of them waited until her footsteps had gone. Then Reynolds doubled up with helpless laughter. He was crouched over his mirth like pain. When he had finally recovered he said, "Jason, you worst man by far. Worst. One day you kill me."

Jason looked on calmly as Reynolds and Ez finally became sober.

Reynolds' face took on a more serious expression. "How we going to deal wid this problem, man?"

He glanced at the other two, but neither Ez nor Jason spoke.

CHAPTER 12

At Ez's flat, the movement of cutlery on plates sounded loud.

Steve sat silently at the other end of the table, eating his salt fish and ortanique curry with a detached diligence. He was taller than Ez by several inches, slimmer. When he smiled, his grin was lopsided. He had something of an athlete's grace.

Ez said, "So how you likin' your job?"

Steve's expression became cautious, almost sullen.

"OK."

"You not training at de club any more?"

"Don't have time."

Ez was aware of a faint movement from Martha's hands, a sign of restlessness or unease. He knew she hated confrontations between the two of them. Her expression pleaded for sympathy. Ez glanced at her, then at Steve again.

"Why you choose hairdressin'?"

Steve shrugged. "Work."

"Don't sound like good work to me."

Martha said, "Seems like good work to me."

Ez ignored her.

"You chasin' white girls, maybe?"

Steve glanced briefly upward in frustration. He looked at Martha, then back at his plate.

Ez ignored the interchange of glances between them. He said, "How much you getting?"

"Eighty-four pound a week basic wages," Steve said.

Ez was silent.

"Plus maybe a hundred and thirty pounds in tips."

"One hundred and thirty pound!"

Ez was incensed. At the other end of the table Steve seemed to float in his own air, detached. He held his own ground, staring back.

Martha said, "He can help us with things."

"One hundred thirty pound?"

Martha pleaded, "He talented. He got prospects. Been there only a few weeks now."

Steve glanced again at Martha, then back at Ez.

"You want me to move out?"

Ez ate silently for several minutes. Martha, not daring to speak, picked over her own salt fish and rice.

✻

In the Gents the quality of the light seemed to change in the afternoon. It became thick, like mist or fog. Sometimes it seemed to suck the atmosphere out.

Ez mopped the floor. He looked around at the long line of urinals.

Customers were entering and leaving. Two men

stood drying their hands at the air-dryers. Another man was leaving the urinal, zipping himself up. It all seemed peaceful.

In Reynolds' office, when they gathered for lunch, Reynolds was almost sombre as he ate his sandwiches.

On the other side of the table, Jason dipped his ryebread into his I-tal vegetarian food and chewed contemplatively. He sipped his tea. The two of them – Reynolds and Jason – purveyed an almost ferocious private concentration.

Reynolds said, "How many more reptiles we got to trow out before we satisfy de council?"

Jason paused in his eating. He said, "Too many."

The three of them were attuned to the sounds in the Gents outside the door – the hesitant mechanism of the turnstiles as a customer entered, the movement of footsteps to the urinals, the pause at the tiled face, the returning footsteps, and then the more sudden and decisive rattle of the turnstile on departure. The pattern was so constant that they almost did not notice it.

There were other sounds too, of cubicle doors opening and closing. It seemed to Ez that a few days after Reynolds' and Jason's violence, the population had returned to its former niche.

Jason said, "I'm seeing it dis way. Up to now, we living in some kind of ecological balance wid de reptiles. Dis place is like a swamp. Trow out one reptile, another come."

Ez looked from one to the other. The intensity of their discussion faintly amused him.

Reynolds and Jason continued to eat their food, pondering the ways of the world.

After a while, Reynolds said to Jason, "What you tinkin', man?"

Jason was silent.

Reynolds repeated, "Whaffor you?"

"Nuttin', man."

"You de worse man in de worl'," Reynolds said with approval. "When it come to evil, no one like you."

Jason drank his tea and belched softly. "I'm tinkin' maybe we have to drain de swamp."

Reynolds paused in his eating. No one impressed him in strategic thought quite like Jason. Reynolds smiled covertly at Ez.

Ez seemed about to say something, but Reynolds put a finger to his lips to enjoin silence.

Jason said, "De way I see it, de reptiles don' like bein' observed."

They watched him.

"Maybe now. Maybe now we persuade dem dey bein' watched."

Reynolds eyes narrowed in concentration.

"How, man?"

"Maybe now, we need sign."

"What sign you talkin'?"

"Sometin' official, man. 'Observation cubicle', maybe."

"What you sayin'?"

Reynolds had caught a small spark of Jason's intent.

"You bringing in de police?"

"No police, man."

"Who doin' de surveyin'?"

"No one surveyin', man. Just a sign."

"A sign of what?" Reynolds asked.

Jason said, "Sign alone."

"Where, man?"

"On one of de cubicles."

"One of de cubicles?" Reynolds asked. "Which one?"

"Any one, man."

There was a brief pause while Reynolds considered.

"Who making dese signs?"

"Harry," Jason said. "Down Chiswick, maybe."

"Big Harry?"

Jason nodded.

"You tinkin', man." Reynolds said. "You tinkin'."

✳

On Sunday Ez and Martha, dressed in their best clothes, sat in the congregation of the Second Adventist Church. The men were in dark suits, the women wore hats. Their pastor, Hosanna Davies, addressed them from the pulpit. He was Jamaican in origin, but they said he was also one-quarter Welsh. His basso stirred the air of the hall above them.

"If I steal one apple, one tiny apple, from a fruit merchant's stall, what have I done?" Pastor Davies asked the congregation. "I have stepped across the line into evil, and once I have stepped across that line what is there to prevent me going further? What is there, I ask myself, to prevent me setting deeper into the darkness? When we leave the light, all darkness is our darkness. If I have stolen an apple, what is it that separates me from the common criminal who steals for his living, or from the mugger and the murderer? Only a matter of degree."

"Amen," the congregation said.

"Once we have crossed the dark river into the shadow of evil, we are lost sheep. Therefore let none of us do other than remain in virtue, and do no evil. For once evil lays its hand upon you, the path back to the fold is narrow and difficult, and you shall not easily reach home again."

"Praise be the Lord," the congregation said.

"Let us help those of us who are drawn to the easy way, who lower their guard against evil. Except as you shall lay your hand upon the shoulder of another in friendship, be wary of what is promised to you, or of what is expected. For many a man has been drawn to evil by an easy indifference to the behaviour of his neighbours."

When the collecting pouch came to Ez and Martha, Ez put in a five-pound note before passing it on to the next man.

As Ez and Martha emerged from their worship, arm in arm, Pastor Davies was standing outside the red-brick building.

"How you, Ez?"

"Fine, Pastor, fine."

"And you, Martha?"

"Pretty good."

"My wife thanks you for the church flowers."

"Pleasure," Martha said.

Pastor Davies leaned amiably and conspiratorially towards Ez. "I notice you put five pound in the collection. You back in work?"

Ez nodded. "Found another job."

"Praise be. You lucky. Plenty people out of work today."

"Unemployment terrible ting."

"There are tribulations in store for all of us," Pastor Davies said. "Beware the adder beneath thy feet."

Ez pointed to his eye. "Keepin' my eye on de reptile."

"Good man." Pastor Davies nodded sagely. "Goodbye now."

Ez and Martha moved on. Another couple approached the minister.

❋

At lunch Ez asked, "Where Stevie today?"

"Out with friends," Martha replied.

"What kind of friends dis boy keep?"

"Come on," Martha said, "he allowed his own friends." She ate and smiled. "How's your own work? Happy?"

"Is OK. Mr Reynolds and Jason, they fixing to drain the swamp."

"Drain the swamp?"

"Keep away de reptiles."

"What reptiles?"

"The perverts."

Martha ate her food without commenting.

"You help them?"

Ez ate for a little while, lost in thought.

"Those two ..." Ez shook his head. "They don't need help. Always up to no good." He smiled to himself. "That Jason."

In their bedroom that night, undressing, Martha

changed into her shift, approached him from behind, and embraced him.

"Thank you for being so good about Stevie."

Ez smiled, though he was beset by conflicting thoughts. He turned to embrace Martha. She was flirtatious. She giggled at his sudden, unexpected fervour.

"Where you coming from, man?"

Embracing each another, they moved sideways towards the bed.

Afterwards, Martha exhaled a heavy sigh of satisfaction. Ez's face, happy, smiled up at her.

Martha dismounted and lay alongside him, face against his cheek, watching him in profile.

Martha said, "You thinking?"

Ez glanced around the room, at the wardrobe that he had assembled, and the mahogany commode they had brought over from her parents' house in Mandeville. Her father had been a senior clerk in a law firm. Sometimes Ez wondered whether he had been worthy of her.

"I'm thinking about that place I work."

Martha brought her hand to his cheek and stroked it.

"What you thinking?" she asked.

"What shock me most of all about de reptiles."

She paused. "What?"

"Not what they do, man."

"What, then?"

He tried to express something.

"Their courting."

"What you mean?"

Ez said, "No beginning at all. No flirtation, just straight down to it. Nothing afterward. Once it over, dey out, man, like a shot from a gun. Don' say nothing to each another. Don' see dem, maybe ever again."

"That what shock you?"

Ez gazed into the darkness.

"What about men with prostitutes?" Martha asked. "No preliminary. No see again afterward. That shock you too?"

He wanted to argue, to say that between men and prostitutes there was often courtship involved – of a strange and perfunctory kind, admittedly. He wanted to say that men looked for different things from prostitutes, sometimes only to talk, sometimes simply the comfort of an embrace. He wanted to say that most men visited the same prostitute again. Above all, he wanted to tell her that she didn't know about the atmosphere of the Gents, the sense of lust alone, the strange smell of waste and implacable metals.

"You not answerin'," Martha said.

Instead he said, "You right again." He was surprised at the comfort this admission gave him, like obeisance to a deity. Afterwards, he was able to slip with perfect equanimity into sleep.

CHAPTER 13

The following day Ez stood at the frame of one of the cubicles, looking in through the open door.

Jason was standing inside, indicating something with his hands.

"Look at dis, man."

Jason pointed to a hole that had been drilled in one of the partition walls dividing one cubicle from another. Ez edged his way around the door so he could see better. The aperture was about three feet from the floor, two inches in diameter, and approximately circular.

"Look, man."

Jason put his finger through the hole and wiggled it.

"Spyhole?" Ez asked.

"No, man. I show you."

Jason made as if he were unzipping himself. He put his midriff at the hole.

"Sometin' else, man."

Ez turned away, attempting to hide his laughter.

Jason pressed his midriff to the hole, rolling his eyes.

"Reptile on de other side lovin' it, man."

Reynolds was a few minutes late that morning. He appeared at the turnstile and waved to Ez. Ez, still shaking with laughter, walked over, pressed a red button on the inner side of the turnstile, and let Reynolds through.

In his right hand Reynolds carried a blue plastic shopping bag. He glanced in at Jason in the cubicle and shook his head.

Somewhat shamefacedly, Jason removed himself from his position.

Reynolds unlocked his office door.

"Come see what I got."

Ez and Jason followed Reynolds into his office. Reynolds removed his overcoat and hung it up. He reached into the shopping bag and pulled out a small engraved sign in black on white lettering.

Ez and Jason looked down at it. It read: OBSERVATION CUBICLE. PRIVATE.

Reynolds reached into the carrier bag again and removed a video camera and a mounting frame. He placed them on the table.

Jason said, "What dis cost you?"

"Three pound, man. Broken down observation video. Nuttin' work inside. Bought it from second-hand shop in Balls Pond road."

Reynolds picked up the video camera and trained it on Jason.

"What you think?"

"Sometin' else, man," Jason said.

"We put it up soon."

Reynolds set the video camera down on the table

and pulled out of his carrier bag a screwdriver and a packet of screws.

"For fitting."

They considered the objects laid out on the table. After a few moments Reynolds said, "I have to finish my weekly accounts for Mrs Steerhouse."

Jason nodded.

Reynolds sat down at the desk and began to add figures on a calculator.

They knew they were dismissed. Jason gathered the television camera and its mount into his arms. Ez picked up the screwdriver and screws. They went out, closing the door. Reynolds seemed hardly to notice their departure.

＊

Jason screwed the sign onto the door of cubicle five. Ez attended, handing him each of the corner screws in turn. Afterwards Jason stood back and admired the small sign with its air of discreet officialdom.

Jason unlocked the door of the large store-cupboard at the end of the room. They hauled a tall aluminium step-ladder into position beneath the main roof beam. Jason ascended the ladder and tapped the beam with the screwdriver. There was a hollow, metallic clang of steel.

After a brief consultation they decided not to disturb Reynolds. Jason was about to set out to buy some steel drills when he glanced up at the ceiling again. On a part of the beam closest to Reynolds' office door was a heavy wooden board. It had once served as the backing to a fuse-box. Subsequently the fuse-box had been relocated to the interior of Reynolds' office.

They shifted the step-ladder under the board and Jason ascended again. He used one arm both to brace himself against the ceiling and to pin the camera mount against the wooden board. With his other hand he began to screw the mount to the wood. There were eight screws in all and it took nearly ten minutes. He fixed the camera in place, tightened the final two screws, and looked along the lens's line of sight. The camera position was several feet higher than the uppermost part of the cubicles.

Jason climbed down the ladder and knocked on Reynolds' door. A few moments later Reynolds set aside his accounts and emerged to inspect Jason's work. He paused at the sign on the cubicle door and then checked the alignment of the camera.

"You think dis legal?" Jason asked. "Puttin' observation camera above de cubicle?"

"Line of sight only allow you see heads," Reynolds said. "Man sit down, no see."

"Decent, maybe?" Jason asked.

Reynolds nodded. "Decent, I'm tinkin'."

He glanced at his watch. "Time to open de swamp."

Reynolds disappeared back into his office to work at his accounts. Ez lifted the empty collecting box off Reynolds' desk and walked to the turnstiles to unlock the steel side-door. He fitted the collecting box into place and locked it, then used the second key on the ring to unlock the paying mechanism on the turnstiles.

CHAPTER 14

Ez scrubbed the floors at one end of the room. Kneeling, he moved backward with the brush gripped in both hands. Jason had taught him how to balance himself on his knees so there was less strain on his back. He had shown Ez how to swing the brush to and fro, holding it two-handed, swaying the torso in rhythm, using his body as a locus of movement, distributing the weight more widely into his forearms and wrists. After a series of sweeps, Ez raised himself, pushed backward the rubber mat that prevented the knees of his overalls from getting dirty, and began to work the floor again with the brush.

He became oblivious of time. The feet and legs of various men passed by him as he scrubbed, but he concentrated on the area of his work.

At the other end of the room, Jason had put in his earphones and was mopping the floor with a long-handled mop. He seemed unaware of anything but the music itself. Sometimes he jerked and moved in a syncopated way. The earphones gave off a faint, scratchy hissing. In an interval between traffic Ez thought he heard the cheerful strains of Bob Marley's "Africa Unite!", on another occasion the heavier, thudding beat of "Iron Lion Zion".

❋

It was Ez who saw the man first. He was short, square, with a carefully manicured beard that framed his mouth. He approached one of the wash-basins opposite the cubicles and began to wash his hands.

Ez glanced around. Jason was at the other end of the room, mopping the floor. He moved the mop in large figures of eight, swinging his body around so that sometimes he faced directly away, twitching occasionally to the music in his earphones. Ez walked over to the wall and carefully cleaned the floor brush, waiting his opportunity to catch Jason's attention.

Jason pivoted gently to the music. Ez, out of the corner of his eye, saw Jason give a slight nod in the direction of the man.

Ez smiled to himself at Jason's percipience. He cleaned the tags and fluff from the floor brush, then rinsed it with hot water. Vapour rose around him. He smelt the traces of the accumulated ammonia and disinfectant. Through the cloud of steam he glanced down the room again.

The man had finished washing his hands. In the same, creamy trance he put his hands under one of the air-dryers. On his way out, he turned and moved towards the cubicles as if he were about to enter one. Then he paused, transfixed, in front of the sign which read: OBSERVATION CUBICLE. PRIVATE.

Something seemed to grow still inside him. His eyes glanced swiftly round the room, as though searching for a potential attacker. They lighted on the newly installed video camera.

The man's attention shifted swiftly towards Ez and Jason. For a moment, the three of them seemed like animals in a clearing who have just recognised one another's presence. The man pivoted away from the cubicles and walked through the turnstiles.

❋

At lunchtime Ez, Reynolds, and Jason ate their sandwiches. Steaming cups of tea stood beside their lunch boxes.

Reynolds drew out a fresh sandwich and bit into it.

"So, what new, Jason?"

Jason paused while he sipped his tea.

"Reptile coming in," Jason said. "Seein' de new equipment."

Reynolds said, "What doin'?"

"Eyeballing de place."

"Anytin' else?"

Jason took several mouthfuls. "Heading for de hills like de scalded cat."

"Tol' you, man," Reynolds said. "Reptile got big fear."

It seemed to them there was already a different rhythm to the movement and slamming of cubicle doors. Usually, when they left the room for their lunch in Reynolds' office, doors began to open and close more often, as though the occupants had been waiting for their temporary departure before moving to the cubicle of their choice. Now the urinal seemed curiously quiet.

In the silence Ez said, "My wife, Martha, ask me to invite you both to our place for dinner."

"Dinner?" Reynolds asked.

"Some night soon."

"Kind woman," Reynolds said graciously. "Invite Jason too?"

"Both of you, and your misses."

"Jason, what you say?" Reynolds asked. "Which wife you bring, man?"

Jason appeared noncommittal. Reynolds said, "Jason, you worst man." To Ez, Reynolds said, "You put Jason in quandary."

Ez said, "Bring whoever you like, Jason, man."

Reynolds rocked on his chair with laughter. Jason looked bemused.

"What de problem, Jason? You got tree wives now?"

Jason refused to be drawn. After a few moments, Ez said, "Martha suggest next Thursday."

Reynolds pulled a small diary out of his pocket and consulted it. "Fine with me."

"Jason?" Ez asked.

"Fine, man."

"Who you bring with you, man?"

"Maybe one," Jason said, "maybe another."

"You terrible man, Jason," Reynolds said. "De very worst. Never seen anytin' like it."

✳

The silence of the cubicles seemed to extend into the afternoon.

At five o'clock Reynolds emerged from the office, checked his watch and the wall clock, and walked to the turnstiles. He hauled the iron grille across, pulled the heavy padlock from his pocket, snapped it into position, and locked the grille.

Reynolds walked to the turnstile, pulled another key from his pocket, unlocked a small metal gate, opened it, and slid out the metal cash collector. He closed the gate, locked it, and carried the cash collector through to his office.

Inside the office Reynolds opened the wall safe, put the cash collector inside the safe, closed it, spun the combination.

When Reynolds emerged from his office, closing and locking the door, Ez and Jason were waiting to leave.

Reynolds unlocked the side-door, followed the

others through to the exterior, and locked the door behind him.

The three of them walked up a flight of steps to the street. At the top of the stairs, Reynolds said, "Another day, man."

"So long," Ez said.

They departed their separate ways into the dusk.

CHAPTER 15

At Ez's flat, the doorbell rang. Ez walked through the hallway to the front door and opened it.

Reynolds, in a navy-blue jacket, was standing outside with his wife.

"Come in, come in."

Reynolds said, "My wife, Emily."

She was almost as tall as Reynolds, but where Reynolds appeared as aloof as an undertaker, there was something more nervous, alert, in her disposition. She wore white gloves against the cool November air. Ez smiled and shook hands with her. He guided them into the sitting-room.

"Come through. Martha in the kitchen."

Reynolds glanced around at the furniture, the rattan chairs, the lounge suite made in heavy offa wood. "Nice place, man."

They sat down on the sofa.

Martha appeared, taking off oven mittens. Reynolds stood up and shook hands with her.

"Martha," Ez said. "Mr Reynolds. His wife Emily."

Martha said, "Heard plenty about you."

The doorbell rang. Ez said, "Excuse me."

Jason was in a green, red, and gold caftan, flanked by his two women. He reminded Ez more than ever of an Ethiopian prince.

"Jason, man."

Ez briskly embraced him and turned to the two women. Jason introduced them.

"Meryl ..." Ez shook hands with a tall young black woman, whose smile opened like a flower.

"From Kingston?"

"Trench Town," Meryl said.

"Latouké," Jason said. Ez shook hands with a handsome, copper-skinned woman in a blue-and-white robe.

"Some fine name. Where you from?"

"Guinea Bissau."

Ez glanced at Jason. He had always assumed Jason would pick his women from Jamaica, probably from the Rasta community, but clearly he was inclined to range more widely. He winked at Jason and ushered them through.

❋

The first course was peppered shrimps with mango, followed by jerked pork with breadfruit and callaloo. They managed to seat all seven of them at the dining-room table.

The side-table was also piled high with food. They were half way through their first course when Martha, touching a heaped serving dish, said, "More for you, Latouké?"

Latouké declined graciously.

Ez said, "Come on, you got to eat. Emily?"

Emily smiled and held her plate out. Ez loaded her plate until she withdrew it. "Enough? Jason?"

Jason nodded and held his plate out. Martha, closest to him, did the honours. As she spooned cassava onto his plate, Martha said casually, "What all dis I hear about reptiles at work?"

The table became silent. Ez had the impression that the air had been removed between them.

"Reptiles?" Reynolds asked casually. He raised his head and faced Martha directly. His expression was equivocal. Ez deduced immediately that this was not a subject he normally discussed with his wife.

Ez glanced at Jason, but Jason's face was taciturn, withdrawn.

Martha finished spooning food. Jason nodded his head and withdrew his filled plate.

Martha said, "Where you workin'. All de perverts."

Ez looked round at the other women, at the mild

confusion on their faces and their attentive stares. Gently he put his hand on Martha's wrist.

"Martha ..."

Martha said, "I want to know. We all mature people roun' dis table."

Only half jokingly, Reynolds said to Ez, "What you been telling her, man?"

Ez decided to make a clean break. "Bout de people using de establishment."

Ez watched Reynolds reach a certain conclusion, the same clear decision to commit himself that Reynolds had made the day a man threatened Ez with a knife. Reynolds' mouth became a single firm line. He turned to his wife. "I ever speak to you about this?"

Emily shook her head. She turned to Martha.

"Tell me more."

"You haven't tol' her?" Martha asked.

Reynolds smiled, an expression of omission. The atmosphere had lightened a little; perhaps some of the initial shock had worn off.

"Maybe not," Reynolds said. "Maybe you tell us."

He glanced at Ez and returned to eating his food.

Ez removed his hand from Martha's wrist.

Martha said, "Where they work, all these perverts are comin' in de place."

Reynolds had regained his sense of humour. "Dat say it all, man."

Martha persisted. "Using cubicles for sex with other men."

Emily had stopped eating.

In between mouthfuls, Reynolds said to the table at large: "We spendin' half de time keeping de reptiles at bay. Got instruction from de council. Our place traditional meetin' place. Always had bad reputation. Tol' to clean up our act."

Latouké breathed out, as though woken from a dream. "That's terrible. What do you have to do?"

Reynolds said, "Jason, he leadin' de charge. He don' like de reptiles."

Jason had been eating his food quietly. Now he seemed to rise from his own depths, "Nuttin' to do with reptiles. To do with Whitey."

"Whitey?" Martha asked.

In the silence, Reynolds glanced at Ez. There was amusement, but also discomfort, in his expression.

"Whitey cold," Jason said. "Cold inside." He began to utter the dark poetry in his soul. "Colder than reptile. Don' have no emotions. Come to de Gents for de sex wid another reptile. Don' come for de wife, don' want family, maybe don' even want de other man. Come. Afterward go."

Martha glanced round the table.

"You really feel this way, Jason?" Martha asked.

"I feel it, man."

"No black folks come to dis place?"

"Sometime maybe. But black folks is de exception."

"But surely," Martha said, "every one of us is different. Got nuttin' to do with de skin."

"Whitey different," Jason assured her. "Different under de skin."

"Jason," Reynolds said. "You Black Panther, or sumptin'?"

Martha glanced at Ez, but Ez merely shrugged and said, "Jason feel strongly."

"Maybe he does," Martha replied.

In the silence, Ez said, "So what do you think of Arsenal, man, comin' up from behind?"

There was a burst of laughter around the table at the unintentional double entendre. Ez, pleased that he had caused amusement, laughed with the others. The tension lightened again.

It seemed to Ez that he carried the alarmed silence after Jason's speech into the Gents the following day. As he moved back into his work and the voices and clattering utensils grew fainter in his mind, he remembered Jason's conversation with greater clarity.

CHAPTER 16

Reynolds put his head around the door of the manager's office and said to Ez, "Mrs Steerhouse phone up. She comin' today. Ten thirty. You let her in?"

Ez nodded. He was scrubbing out the lavatory bowls with his brush, replacing toilet rolls. He moved from cubicle to cubicle. Apart from the occasional customer, the cubicles were empty of traffic. When he had finished the toilet bowls, he concentrated on cleaning and shining the stainless steel handles of the cisterns.

Perhaps half an hour later he noticed Mrs

Steerhouse trying to attract his attention behind the turnstiles. He gestured to the side-door.

Mrs Steerhouse disappeared from the turnstile. Ez unbolted the side-door from the inside.

"Morning, Mrs Steerhouse."

"Morning, Mr Murphy."

Mrs Steerhouse wore a cardigan against the cold. He caught the faint scent of eau-de-Cologne. Ez knocked on Reynolds' door. Reynolds appeared, a calculator in one hand. There was something courtly and almost flirtatious in his manner.

"Come in, Mrs Steerhouse. You like some tea?"

"Wouldn't say no."

"You have your figures to lecture me?"

"I think so," Mrs Steerhouse said. "Have you yours?"

"Believe so."

The door closed.

Ez returned to scrubbing the lavatories.

✳

A few minutes later, Reynolds appeared again at the door. He gestured for Ez and Jason to come in.

Ez put down his cleaning cloth in the pail, pulled off his rubber gloves, and set the pail against the wall. He entered Reynolds' office. Jason followed, drifting in his own time.

Mrs Steerhouse was seated at the table. Reynolds appeared less than his usual affable self. He gestured to Ez and Jason to sit down.

When Jason and Ez had taken their places, Reynolds said, "Mrs Steerhouse got something to tell us."

Mrs Steerhouse turned to Ez and Jason. "Mr Reynolds and I have been going through the figures. I was asked to make a visit because over the last month or so there has been a marked drop in revenue from the turnstiles. Close to a forty per cent drop, in fact."

They watched her carefully.

"Naturally, it is my duty to check up on whether the income is properly accounted for, but the machine totals match up to income. Mr Reynolds has been able to confirm that these are the precise totals from the machines."

She paused.

"In your opinion, what would you gentlemen say is responsible for the sharp fall in revenue?"

Ez and Jason glanced at each other. They both looked at Reynolds for guidance, but Reynolds merely nodded to them.

Ez cleared his throat. "Reduction in de reptiles, maybe."

"Sorry, Mr Murphy?" Mrs Steerhouse's tone was sharp. "Reptiles?"

Ez glanced at Reynolds again. Reynolds nodded.

Ez said, "De cottagers."

A brief silence followed. Mrs Steerhouse said, "The cottagers?"

She looked at Reynolds.

Reynolds said, "Mrs Steerhouse, what Ez mean is

that you tell us to reduce de number of de cottagers."

"Yes ..."

"We followin' orders."

Mrs Steerhouse paused. She swallowed once and considered what she had heard.

"Are you saying that cottagers amounted to forty per cent of the total traffic of this establishment?"

"Sometin' like that," Reynolds said.

Jason said, "Maybe more, maybe less."

Mrs Steerhouse looked from Reynolds to Jason. "Good God."

"Dis place famous for it," Reynolds said. "Always have been. De cottagers comin' from miles around."

Mrs Steerhouse seemed to take in a deep breath.

"But that's awful." She considered for several seconds. "You see, if these reduced turnstile revenues continue for a further two months, I have been told by my superiors that we can only afford two personnel at this establishment. One of you will have to go."

Out of the ensuing silence, Reynolds said, "Mrs Steerhouse. We following your instructions. We do our best to eliminate de reptiles – de cottagers. Now, because we successful, you tinkin' maybe sackin' one of us."

"Mr Reynolds, you must understand that I too am following instructions ..."

Jason, who had kept largely silent, leaned forward.

"Mrs Steerhouse ..."

Mrs Steerhouse paused in mid-sentence. "Yes?"

"I'm tinkin'. Maybe the authorities must make up their mind."

"What do you mean?"

"We have reptiles and good revenue, or we have no reptiles and de low revenue."

"That's one way of looking at it, certainly. I'm not sure the authorities would choose to see the matter in quite that light."

"You want us to open up de swamp again for de reptiles, we open up de swamp." Jason said. "I tink dis is your decision."

"Well, I think we've aired these matters

sufficiently. I'll report back to my superiors on the council." She paused. "In the meantime, I must thank you gentlemen for the tea."

Mrs Steerhouse rose. The three of them stood up. Reynolds opened the door for her and walked with her until she exited through the turnstiles.

"Goodbye, Mr Reynolds."

Reynolds watched her walking up the stairs, then returned to the office and closed the door. He seemed locked in his own thoughts. Ez sensed the weight of silence between the other two.

Jason said, "I do wrong?"

Reynolds shook his head.

"No, man. You tellin' de truth."

Reynolds sat down. He looked across at Jason. "You hear what she say?"

"I hear, man."

Reynolds seemed physically diminished. At the same time a kind of restlessness seized him. After a few moments he stood up and walked around the room. Ez watched him pause at the skylight, staring up into the grey afternoon light. After a while, Reynolds said, "Last come, first out. Maybe after two month, Ez have to go."

Ez nodded. He felt a dryness in his throat. He was surprised by his own anger. He stared at Reynolds' back.

Without warning Jason interceded, "No, man, I go first."

Reynolds turned towards Jason.

"Way I look at it," Jason said, "it me who suggest we drain de swamp."

"But we all agreed, man."

Ez nodded.

"Second ting," Jason continued. "I been in dis work five, maybe six years. Been saving some money for a flight back to Jamaica."

"You serious?" Reynolds asked.

"Been putting de two women out to work. Meryl receptionist, Letouké pharmacist. We all got savings, man, we all ready now go back to Kingston."

"Dey agree?" Reynolds asked.

"Dey follow me, man. We set up small shop, general store. Got de capital. Nuttin' hold us back."

Reynolds sat down and faced Jason. "You sure?"

Jason nodded.

Reynolds said, "I miss you, man. De wors' I ever met. Bar none."

"Tell you sometin'," Jason continued. "I tired of being with Whitey. Everywhere I go, Whitey there. Mrs Steerhouse come, tell us dis place close down unless we trow out reptile; trow out reptile, give one of us de sack." They noticed the high singsong, the rhythm of his conviction. Jason paused. "I go now. Ez keep his job. Best time for me."

"Jason, man ..."

"Want to live with my own kind."

Reynolds considered him for what seemed a long time. Then he breathed out in acceptance. "We miss you, man."

"Maybe you come to Kingston, sometime."

Reynolds nodded, but he was depressed. "When you goin'?"

"Couple weeks time, maybe."

"You move fast, man."

"I make up my mind."

"When?" Reynolds asked.

"When what?"

"When you make up your mind?"

Jason paused. "Ez's party, maybe."

Reynolds nodded, as though in melancholy confirmation of a truth already known. He glanced at Ez, who sensed the faint stirrings of the landslide, the progressive collapse of Reynolds' inner world.

CHAPTER 17

When Ez was young, an old obeah at Greenwich Farm, Fat Lion Stevens, had taught him how to lie suspended on the edge of sleep, how to use the rhythm of his breathing to cast his mind back and forth. The obeah had used the image of swinging like a bird on a thin branch – "Bird always upright, bird never fall" – allowing his spirit to range out from his body.

Lying in his bed, awake, staring at the ceiling, Ez found himself sometimes subject to visions. Martha slept beside him, facing away, snoring peacefully. He breathed the fragrance of the cedarwood dressers.

When he half closed his eyes, he imagined himself working at the urinals with a wrench, making sure that the fittings were tight, checking for leaks.

The obeah had said that was how you recognised your own spirit in dream states, by the familiarity of its actions. It was like a dog. It did something that was familiar to you before setting off on its wanderings.

While Ez dreamed, he saw a young man walk into one of the adjacent cubicles, moving lightly and almost soundlessly.

Ez tightened a valve with the wrench, turned round, and caught a glimpse of the back of another man entering the same cubicle. The door closed calmly. He heard nothing more.

His spirit became mordant and unsettled by the closeness of the silence, the way it seemed to rise up over the door and drift like vapour across the floors. He put down the wrench, stood up, moved across to Reynolds' office, knocked on Reynolds' door. He heard no reply and entered.

Inside the office Reynolds was nowhere to be seen. Ez crossed the floor to the camera, which hung from a hook on the wall. He took down the camera, turned towards the door, and left the office with the camera in hand.

He knocked on the door of the cubicle and stood back. There was no sound or sign of movement. He looked up and down the deserted urinal.

Without warning the door opened, and the first man walked calmly towards the turnstiles.

A short while later, the second man walked out casually and made his way to the exit. Ez followed them, raising the camera. Neither man seemed to notice his presence. He pursued them through the turnstiles and up the stairs.

At the top, the first of the men turned to the right, the second to the left.

There was a moment when both men seemed to have disappeared. Ez walked past a bus shelter and came face to face with the second man. He was standing with his arm around a woman. The woman was holding the handle of a large black pram, one of those Victorian prams which seem as large as a coffin. She was rocking it slowly back and forth.

She said softly to the man, "You took your time."

Ez approached them and halted. The woman glanced at his camera, then at Ez's face. The man looked on with a strange mixture of imperturbability and pleading.

Ez stared from her face to the man's, then back again. The woman suddenly appeared concerned for him. It was Ez who was embarrassed, who smiled a brief smile.

The woman said, "Can we help you?"

Ez shook his head, unable to speak.

Still considering him, the woman moved the pram backward and forward. Ez felt a compulsion to look inside it. He saw Reynolds' face. Reynolds was lying on his back and was gently sleeping. His cheekbones were white; he seemed composed.

"You sure?" the woman asked.

Ez glanced at the man, then back at her. He

nodded again. He took a step backward, turned, and departed. As he left, he heard the woman say in a voice that combined perplexity and concern, "Who was that?"

Ez descended the steps to the Gents. Before he reached the turnstiles he halted, breathed out, and leaned against the wall in consternation.

In the bedroom, Ez took deep breaths and opened his eyes. He turned slowly in the darkness, glanced at Martha peacefully sleeping, then stared at the ceiling again.

CHAPTER 18

A few days later Ez and Jason were mopping the floor, moving in unison down the room with about five feet between them. Jason had his earphones on. As they moved past the cubicles, Ez heard a sigh, and then a faint drubbing, scuffling sound, like a spin dryer.

Jason, impervious to outside sounds, showed no sign of hearing it. Ez pointed toward the nearest cubicle.

Jason nodded and carefully removed his headphones.

The cubicle seemed to shudder slightly.

Ez rapped on the door. Simultaneously, Jason

moved round to the side of the cubicle and gave three heavy punches with the heel of his hand.

They waited in chords of descending silence.

Suddenly the door of the cubicle opened. A tall man in his early twenties strode briskly out and through the turnstiles almost before Ez or Jason had a chance to react.

Jason glanced at Ez, half amused.

The abandoned cubicle was silent. Carefully, as if stalking a dangerous animal, Jason reached out toward the door. His fingers touched the wooden surface, then pushed it open. The hinges creaked briefly. Jason stood back against the possibility of a frightened charge towards the turnstiles.

The door swung back freely and struck the inner surface of the cubicle with a hollow bang.

A tall, elegant black man in a leather jacket emerged. He did not avoid eye contact. With a calm arrogance, he considered them both. Then, having made his assessment, he walked with unruffled poise toward the turnstiles.

Ez and Jason watched.

It seemed to Ez that Jason was overcome by a kind of compulsion. It drove him into action. He moved swiftly to draw alongside the man and engage him in conversation.

"What you doin' in there, me bredda?"

The man did not reply.

"Kneelin' down in front of Whitey?"

The man walked towards the turnstiles, unperturbed.

Matching calm for calm, Jason appeared almost conversational.

"You like to give him yo' nigger rass? Maybe you offerin' lip service?"

Ez, standing still, watched. They had halted and were standing beside each other like old acquaintances.

"You like music, man? What sorta instrument you playin'? Oboe?"

The man turned slowly, with mogul calm, towards Jason.

"Why you want to know?" he asked at last. "Got some special interest?"

Jason's face smiled, but it was hardly a smile at all, just a shimmer on water.

"Maybe you want to be in there too?" the man suggested.

"All you queens say that, man," Jason said. "Think you can spook me with that talk?"

"What you want me to come up with, truly? Deep inside?"

Jason smiled again, the same shimmering smile. His affability appeared constrained, defined. It seemed he might have been preparing to shake hands and let the matter rest. But without warning, he hit the man hard in the stomach.

Twenty feet away, Ez felt the power of the blow. He watched the man collapse slowly on to his knees. His eyes clouded with pain. In the course of his collapse he did not take his eyes off Jason's eyes. He struggled with his pain, then seemed to compose himself. On his knees, his own eyes shone out with defiance.

After a while the man said, "You enjoy that?"

A brief convulsion of loathing passed across Jason's face. Perhaps he calculated that the man was drawing him into his own game, daring him to walk down a path he could not win. Without a word, Jason turned and walked back down the room.

He went straight by Ez without speaking. Ez turned and looked at the man, who kneeled in profile by the turnstile. The man was staring ahead, softly whispering to himself as if he were praying.

At the other end of the room Jason put on his headphones, apparently oblivious. He picked up his mop and began to sweep the floor again in long strokes.

Near the entrance the man slowly rose. He seemed to breathe in deeply, then turned and walked through the turnstiles. His footsteps receded up the stairs.

Ez considered for several moments the empty staircase beyond the turnstiles.

❋

Later that afternoon, when Ez put down his mop, Jason was still absorbed in his own silence.

During tea, Jason said nothing, despite Reynolds' attempts to josh him. Still uncommunicative at the end of the day, Jason hung up his green overall, put on his overcoat, and slipped a scarf around his neck. Ez looked at Jason, catching his eye.

"You thoughtful, man."

Jason nodded. "Tinkin' about that nigger."

"What about him?"

"I'm tinkin', look what living with Whitey has done to him."

Ez said, "Maybe he chose it for himself."

Jason gave him a brief glance, cold and mercurial. It was as if they realised, finally, that they were on either side of a gap that could not be bridged.

"Maybe," Jason said.

Reynolds appeared from his office with the keys.

He locked his office and then unlocked and opened the side-door. The three of them trooped out. Reynolds slipped the heavy key into the lock and turned the tumblers so that the door was shut and locked behind them.

It seemed to Ez that they were departing like ghosts into the dusk, each on their separate paths, out into the pools of the winter street lights.

CHAPTER 19

A heavy Tristar landed at Heathrow, with a spit and flash of smoke from its wheels.

Ez turned away from the window of the departure lounge. Jason seemed curiously grave, detached, his dreadlocks held in a cap with the Ethiopian colours of red, green, and gold.

Ez briefly embraced Meryl and Latouké.

Reynolds' face was impassive. He had worked six years with Jason, day after day. Now he and Emily stood back like sombre parents at the departure of their son.

"Where you goin' to live?" Ez asked Jason.

"Bull Bay," Jason replied.

"East of Kingston?"

"Near Morant."

Ez nodded.

Jason said, "Close by Cane River Falls."

"You all alone," Ez said. "Mountain villages."

"Good Rasta community."

Ez smiled. "Maybe."

Martha embraced Meryl and Latouké.

They watched Jason and the two women depart, hauling their wheeled cases.

❋

That evening, when Ez and Martha were in bed, Martha asked, "You sorry Jason gone?"

Ez nodded.

Martha said, quoting Jason, "'All Whitey is reptile.' You agree with him?"

"Why you say that?"

"Maybe he got problems."

"Jason sincere," Ez insisted. "Say exactly what he mean."

"Maybe Hitler sincere, too."

"If Jason feel that way, right for him to go back to Jamaica."

"What about the girls?" Martha asked. "Leave good jobs here. Go to live in Rasta community."

"Their decision."

"Serving in some store? Keeping goats in the back yard? Picking yams?"

"Find extra work in San Antonio or Morant Bay, five or ten miles maybe."

"He allow them?"

"Why not?"

Martha said, "Perhaps Jason frightened they desert him. Maybe he lock them up."

Ez smiled. "You know why Jason so successful with women?"

"Why?"

"No fear. One woman goes, another come."

Martha turned away from him and lay on her side.

She said, "One woman comes, another goes."

He laughed at her implacability. But he wanted to tell her something that he had learnt only slowly, by association. He had picked it up through his skin, like heat. He said, "Jason committed to his religion in same way as us, maybe more."

"His women too?"

"You don't understand. Rasta say woman is not possession. Forbid envy."

Martha did not answer. Ez felt an urge to explain. He wanted to tell her Jason's lack of envy was due to a religious injunction, not a lack of character. In the same way, his preference for living in simple rural conditions was not a compromise with circumstance, it was a part of the Rasta ideal, the ascetic life. Above all, he wished to argue that the lack of material things in Jason's new life was not the problem she envisaged but his practical solution to greed.

"You supportin' Jason," Martha said, almost out of sleep.

It was true. Ez wondered what motivated him to

do so. Of what would Jesus approve, he thought – the rejection of material things or their careful, cumulative acquisition? How did you argue that point to a fine, middle-class girl from Mandeville, the daughter of a senior administrative clerk in the legal office of a bauxite-mining company?

Under the spur of Martha's scepticism, Ez tried to work out something in his own mind. He admired Jason not only because he was a Dread but because he also exemplified something Ez understood and approved. Jason was an evocation of the Rastafarian soul. His philosophy counselled that he should do constant good works for his fellow man. It forbade drink. It advocated ascetism and personal discipline. The ganja weed was taken as religious experience, much as some Christians took communion wine with prayers.

Dreads were like the old prophets that wandered the wilderness, holding nothing sacred except the Bible. They were like gnostics or Sufis or other holy men.

"One world," Jason would say, raising his hand in greeting as if to bless. "Smooth runnings," he called out, when he said goodbye.

In the darkness, with Martha breathing softly beside him, an image came to Ez of Jason sitting beside him at lunch in Reynolds' office. He stuffed his cheeks like an animal, but his eating had a natural grace. He observed Jason's Ethiopian profile, the clear line of his forehead and nose, the set of his eyebrows, like the outward indications of some subtle internal grace. He noticed how the light fell on Jason's face in planes. Ez would never forget what he sensed so directly – that he had met in Jason someone flawed and at the same time holy.

CHAPTER 20

After Jason had gone, Reynolds seemed to drift through the day without direction. He became noticeably thinner. His face seemed to become greyer, his hair whiter. The bones of his hands became more prominent. When he took his tea, he would sit kneeling forward in his chair, his knees spread, staring into space. His wrist joints made a severe right angle. The mug of tea hung suspended from his long fingers.

One morning Reynolds turned over a page of his *Sun* and said, "De worl' is full of sex and violence, man. Tings here you wouldn't believe."

Ez looked up, nodded sombrely, and returned to his *Mirror*.

After a few minutes, Reynolds said, "Mrs Steerhouse call on telephone. Say she coming dis afternoon."

"What she say?"

"Say nuttin'."

They both continued to read their newspapers.

Reynolds said, "You remember Jason wid de stick? 'I don't understand, Mrs Steerhouse, what is dis smell?'"

They chuckled. It seemed to Ez that Reynolds had taken on some of Jason's singsong tonality,

"Mrs Steerhouse sniffin' de stick. Him lookin' her in de eye, man. Close by. Right up close."

"That Jason."

They returned to their newspapers and sipped their tea.

In the afternoon Ez, with rubber gloves on, was washing his mopping rags in the sink when he heard his named called. In the mirror above the sink he saw Mrs Steerhouse signalling from the turnstiles.

She wore a black mackintosh and was carrying an umbrella against the rain. In her cheerfulness she seemed more than ever like the matron of an old people's home, both stern and humane. Ez, acknowledging her signal, indicated that she should come round to the side-door.

He slid back the bolts, and Mrs Steerhouse entered. He helped her off with her raincoat and hung it against the wall.

"Is Mr Reynolds in?"

Ez nodded. He knocked on Reynolds' door and felt Mrs Steerhouse's inadvertent breath on the back of his neck. After a few seconds Reynolds appeared.

"Mrs Steerhouse."

"Mr Reynolds. What appalling weather."

Her presence seemed to galvanise Reynolds out of his apathy. He ushered her through.

Ez was about to return to his work, when Mrs Steerhouse said, "I think you better join us, Mr Murphy. What I have to discuss concerns you both."

Ez followed her into Reynolds' office.

Mrs Steerhouse sat down. Reynolds and Ez sat opposite her.

"I'm afraid," Mrs Steerhouse said, "I have some bad news for you both." She paused. "Our figures show that the takings from this establishment have decreased a further ten per cent. Even with a reduced staff of two, it is now running at a loss." She considered them both. "These are difficult times, I'm sure you know. The council is placing its officers under pressure to make economic savings wherever possible. Taking all such factors into account, a meeting was called on Wednesday to discuss this particular issue. The Social Services Committee has decided that the establishment shall be closed in one month's time from today."

She paused, seemed to re-arrange her thoughts, then proceeded. "I know this must be a terrible shock to you both, and frankly it isn't a part of my duties I enjoy."

Reynolds breathed out audibly.

"Mr Reynolds," Mrs Steerhouse continued, "you will receive your statutory rights in terms of three months' severance pay. The Committee asked me to thank you both for your service and to wish you well."

Reynolds leant forward and placed his head in his hands.

Mrs Steerhouse swallowed. "Quite." After a few moments she said, "You know you have my deepest sympathy."

Reynolds continued to sit slumped forwards in his chair.

"Well, I'd best be getting on."

Reynolds did not make his customary move to accompany her to the door. Eventually he raised his head from his hands.

"Mrs Steerhouse."

Mrs Steerhouse turned round at the doorway.

"Yes?"

"Dis my work."

"I know, Mr Reynolds."

"What become of dis place now?" Reynolds asked.

"Well, it'll probably be closed down and boarded up."

"No one use it no more?"

Mrs Steerhouse shook her head.

"In the case of another urinal we closed down a few years ago, a local flower seller approached the council with an offer to rent it and set up a small business there."

"Rent?" Reynolds asked.

"Yes, a nominal rent."

"Nominal?" Reynolds seemed to be following her thoughts doggedly.

Mrs Steerhouse swallowed. "One thousand, perhaps two thousand pounds a year."

"Two thousand a year," Reynolds repeated softly.

Mrs Steerhouse paused to consider him.

"Is there anything else, Mr Reynolds?"

"No."

"Well, I am sorry to be the bearer of bad tidings.

At the end of next month, you will be sent your final payments and your severance pay."

Reynolds rose to his feet. Mrs Steerhouse shook hands with them both.

Reynolds escorted her to the door, but Mrs Steerhouse said, "It's all right. I can find my own way out."

They waited until her footsteps had gone, then Reynolds sank back into his chair.

Outside, the Gents was silent. They could hear the faint hiss of the fountains, but the sound itself seemed to be hollowed out. Reynolds' face appeared to Ez more ascetic than ever. He remembered his dream about the pram.

After a while Ez said, "I go clean de place."

Reynolds nodded without looking at him.

❋

Later that afternoon, at tea, Ez said, "Why you asking her about rent?"

"Nuttin', man," Reynolds said. "I was thinking maybe we can run dis place ourselves."

"Run dis place?"

Reynolds shrugged. "Bad idea, man. If it don't support us now, why it support us on our own?"

After a while Ez said, "I'm making another cup of tea. You want one?"

"I take maybe two," Reynolds replied.

Waiting for the kettle to boil, Ez tapped his fingers on the metal drainer. He handed Reynolds his cup and sat down.

Ez blew across the surface. After a while he said, "What you truly think of de reptiles?"

Reynolds seemed to return from his own thoughts.

"Why you asking?"

Ez shrugged, "Maybe nothing."

"Whyfor, man?"

"I'm tinkin'. Dis place, before we drain de swamp, before we clear de reptiles, dis place supporting three people."

"What you sayin', man?"

A sense of what Ez might be suggesting began to form in Reynolds' expression. He appeared genuinely shocked.

"So wha' man? We put a notice on de wall, 'Reptile welcome'?"

"I'm not saying nuttin', man."

"You say sometin'."

"I'm sayin' we don't have de council on our neck no more. Maybe think again."

"What we calling dis place?" Reynolds insisted. "De reptile farm?"

"Listen," Ez said. "Dis place one time before. Normal people mostly, but also some reptiles. Whaffor reptile harm me? He get on with his life, I get on with mine."

"What you sayin', man?"

"I'm not saying encouragement, man. I'm sayin' toleration."

"Toleration," Reynolds repeated.

Ez sipped his tea.

"I think you bad man," Reynolds said. "I tink you worse than Jason."

"Maybe, man, we go back de way it was before. What my business?"

Reynolds considered him. He paused to dip a biscuit in his tea.

"Where we get two thousand pound rent?"

Ez said, "I'm tinkin', maybe, your severance pay."

Reynolds ate his biscuit. His eyes bulged in disbelief.

Ez said, "I'm tinkin'."

"Jason got nuttin' on you, man," Reynolds said. "You de very worst."

CHAPTER 21

Keeping her eye on the television news, Martha said, "How your day today?"

"Some good news, some bad news."

"What de bad news?" Martha asked.

"De bad news is dey closing down de Gents. In one month."

Martha shifted on the sofa. "What de good news?"

"De good news is de council accept our offer. Rent de place for eight hundred pound a year."

"You pay?"

"Mr Reynolds and me. Fifty-fifty. We run de place."

Martha's eyes turned to Ez as though returning from another place.

"You think it work?"

"I don't know. What else I got?"

"Where you get de money?"

"Council defer rent payment two months. Two months we got."

Martha swallowed, then breathed out softly.

"Maybe good thing we got son with proper job."

"Maybe so," Ez agreed.

CHAPTER 22

In the Gents, Ez began to unscrew the sign which read: OBSERVATION CUBICLE. PRIVATE. He put the four small copper screws in his pocket and collected the tall aluminium step-ladder from the cupboard.

He stood on the highest rung of the ladder and applied the screwdriver to the mounting frame of the camera suspended from the beam in the ceiling. The oak facing board held the screws strongly, forcing him to apply both hands to the handle.

Reynolds emerged from the office and stood at the base of the step-ladder.

"You be careful, man."

Once their initial grip had been broken, each of the screws came out easily. Ez handed the camera and its mounting frame down to Reynolds, who steadied the base of the step-ladder while Ez descended.

Reynolds took a newly engraved sign out of his pocket. It read: UNDER NEW MANAGEMENT. The sign seemed to them like a talisman.

Using the same screws he had withdrawn from the sign saying OBSERVATION CUBICLE. PRIVATE, Ez attached the new sign to the door of Reynolds' office.

When the job was completed, Reynolds and Ez stood back and viewed the clean, empty urinal.

Reynolds nodded. He said, "Back to work, man."

During the morning Ez mopped the floor, then scrubbed out the urinals and replaced the disinfectant cakes. He watched Reynolds drift in and out of the office. If anything, Reynolds' air of preoccupation increased. Later that morning, out of the corner of his eye, Ez observed Reynolds checking the broken paper-towel dispenser. He had never before seen Reynolds engage himself in anything mechanical. In the past Reynolds had always relied on Ez and Jason. His sphere was the office, overseeing, ordering fresh supplies of cleaning fluid, cake, lavatory paper, disinfectant, counting the cash, doing the books. Now Reynolds paused opposite the paper-towel dispenser with a hesitant determination, as though facing a new world.

Ez continued to mop the floor. Occasional figures moved past him. The sounds seemed hollow. Around him the atmosphere was strangely calm, as though time were suspended. Hardly daring to address each other, he and Reynolds worked in a vacuum.

✸

In church that Sunday, Pastor Davies preached through a severe cold.

"So I say to you, 'Who should concern himself

with his brother's sin?' A true Christian should consider his own life first, before he concerns himself with the sins of others."

Ez said, "Amen!"

Martha, suspicious of this excess of zeal, turned her head towards him. Ez smiled briefly at her.

Pastor Davies said, "Let us quote more fully from the Scriptures themselves, Matthew 7, 'Judge not, that ye be not judged.

"'For with what judgement ye judge, ye shall be judged, and with what measure ye mete, it shall be meted to you again.

"'And why beholdest thou the mote that is in thy brother's eye, but considerest not the beam that is in thine own eye?

"'Or how wilt thou say to thy brother, Let me pull the mote out of thine eye; and behold, a beam is in thine own eye?

"'Thou hypocrite, first cast out the beam out of thine own eye, and then thou shalt see clearly to cast out the mote out of thy brother's eye.'"

"Amen!" Ez said again. He liked the raw power of the Gospel, the unexpurgated truths. Martha cast another suspicious look at him.

✸

Ez put on rubber gloves to clean out the sump beneath each urinal. He turned off the water supply on one wall, then he unscrewed each sump and poured the yellowing, putrefying contents into a heavy black bucket. The stench made his eyes water. He had to avert his face. Once or twice he felt like retching. When he had finished one wall he screwed the emptied sumps back into place and turned on the flushing, clean water.

In the course of the morning he moved from wall to wall, turning off the water on each wall, unscrewing the sumps, emptying their contents into a bucket. He lifted the cakes of disinfectant so that he could scour the base, returning the cakes after he had finished.

When he was screwing back the sumps on the third wall, Ez glanced down the room and saw a man washing his hands, casually surveying the doors of the cubicles in the mirror. He wore a grey track suit and trainers. His face was pale. Ez glanced at his internal, concentrated expression. He turned away when the man directed a questioning glance towards him.

The man made no move towards the cubicles, just washed his hands thoroughly, applying soap, turning one hand over the other.

The traffic between the turnstiles and the urinals seemed intermittent. Ez returned to his work, scouring the bases and replacing the cakes of disinfectant. When he looked up again the man had gone.

CHAPTER 23

Sometimes, during the days that followed, Reynolds would walk towards the aluminium-framed skylight that let the only light into the office. He would stare up at the feet and ankles of passers-by. A shop opposite had a blue neon sign. Reynolds would stand there for several minutes, his hands clasped behind his back, rocking slowly backward and forward. Ez wondered what he thought about.

At lunchtime Ez and Reynolds ate their sandwiches.

"Business slow," Reynolds said.

"Sometime, man."

"You know what I'm tinkin'?"

"What, man?"

Reynolds paused to eat his sandwich. "Don't see any reptiles."

Ez nodded.

"Gone to another place, maybe," Ez suggested.

"You think?"

Ez shrugged.

Reynolds drank his tea.

"You don't see none yourself?" Reynolds asked.

"One or two, maybe."

"Reptiles?"

"Floating roun' de place," Ez said. "Casin' de joint."

"You think they come back?"

"I don't know. Maybe just looking."

Reynolds shrugged. He ate his sandwich without looking up.

That evening, as Reynolds was locking the outside door, Ez waited for him at the top of the steps.

Reynolds said, "First week, man."

They shook hands. Reynolds disappeared in the direction of the bus stop.

Ez crossed the road towards the station. He moved down the stairs and into the bowels of the underground station. At the bottom of the steps a busker played a clarinet. He was an old man in a threadbare grey suit that had seen better times. Ez had never put a coin in the paper packet because it seemed impertinent to give money to someone of such manifest distinction. But tonight he reached into his pocket and dropped a pound coin into the small paper bag set out on the floor. The old man looked up almost sharply, as though he were trying to discern what had caused this change of behaviour. Guiltily, Ez stepped onto a train.

❋

Several days later, two men in brown overcoats carried a large parcel down the steps and carefully set it against the wall outside the turnstiles. One of them, the older of the two, attempted to attract Ez's attention.

"Mr Reynolds?"

"Inside," Ez said. He walked to Reynolds' door, knocked, and entered.

Ez said, "You order something?"

Reynolds stood up. He followed Ez out to the turnstiles.

"Mr Reynolds?" The man held out a delivery note and moved his finger across a column on the sheet.

"Sign here, please."

Reynolds glanced at the package leaning against the wall. It was square and substantial. He nodded and signed the delivery slip.

"Want any help with installation?" the man asked.

Reynolds shook his head.

Ez watched the two men depart up the steps. He said, "You don't discuss with your partner?"

"Surprise, man," Reynolds said.

They lifted the object through the turnstiles and set it down against the wall of the office. It weighed perhaps forty pounds. When it was set down, Reynolds pulled back the covering plastic. Ez saw the single word DUREX and beneath that, in smaller letters, Dispenser.

Ez felt an urge to laugh out loud. He wanted to say to Reynolds something that Reynolds had said to him, "You are de worst."

"How many it hold?" Ez asked.

"Four hundred packet, tree to a packet."

Ez shook his head.

"Over one thousand, man," Reynolds said proudly. "Plenty safety."

❋

In Reynolds' office Ez and Reynolds stood in front of the table, looking down at the cash container from the turnstiles.

Reynolds said, as though announcing a formal event, "End of second week."

He turned over the cash container and a silver tide of ten-pence coins slid across the desk.

Ez said, "How much, man?"

"Counter say five hundred ninety-four pounds, twenty pence."

Ez paused and then half smiled.

Reynolds said, "We doin' OK, man. I tink we survive."

CHAPTER 24

On his way home Ez walked into the fruiterers, Headley and Son. There was a small queue of three people ahead of him. When his turn came, he asked for two pounds of mangoes. Mrs Headley, a handsome mulatta, weighed them carefully. She and Ez exchanged glances occasionally, though their conversations were limited to small talk. Having weighed them, she took two further mangoes and held them briefly, a trifle suggestively, together in the palm of her hand. Without taking her eyes from his, she slipped them into the packet.

"With compliments of the house."

Ez said, "Thank you." He felt the blush rising up his neck into his face.

He walked along the street and crossed the road, taking the second right into Letter Lane. He crossed again into Whitegate Road, then walked down a small side-street with perhaps a dozen small shops.

A sign above a shop-front read: HAIRDRESSERS. BIZIOU'S.

Ez paused and looked in. Several women were sitting in chairs, having their hair cut. In its aura of feminine domesticity, the interior reminded him oddly of one of those paintings of a harem he had seen in his youth. Women were everywhere, seated under hairdryers, waiting on chaises longues, reading magazines. In the features of one of the hairdressers attending on them, Ez recognised with a faint shock the casual insouciance of Steve. Fascinated despite himself, Ez paused, looked away, then glanced through the window again.

Steve was cutting the hair of a blonde woman of forty or so. His scissors were aimed precisely. He leant over to concentrate on the cut and the fall of hair.

As Ez watched, one of the male hairdressers, standing next to Steve, drifted over to the sideboard with fluid, sashaying hips. He picked up a fresh pair of scissors and drifted back as though in a trance.

Ez glanced up and down the road again, then walked on.

At the end of the pedestrian precinct he crossed the road, carrying his shopping bag.

In the hallway of the flat Ez, helped by Martha, took off his coat. When she had hung it up, Ez handed her the paper packet.

"Three pound mangoes, like you ask."

"I ask for two."

"Sorry. Must have forgotten."

Martha said, as she took the packet, "You somewhere far off today."

"Steve comin' home dis evening?"

"He tol' me dis morning, he going out with friends."

"What sort of friends he got?"

Martha shrugged her shoulders equably.

"Friends. He old enough to have his own friends."

Ez nodded.

Martha said, "How work today?"

"Fine. I tink we startin' make progress, maybe. Five hundred ninety-four pound dis week from de turnstile."

Martha smiled at him, a slow, rich smile that moved slowly outwards into the edges of her mouth. She hugged him.

"You clever man."

When Martha released him, Ez raised his eyebrows and smiled.

Later, in bed, Martha turned out the side-lamp. She moved to face Ez and observed him in the faint glow of the street lamps.

"Why you ask about Stevie?"

Ez said, "Walkin' past de hairdresser's this evening. Seen de people workin' with Stevie.

One man walkin' like woman, flouncin' about de place."

Martha regarded him. "You think Stevie under bad influence?"

"Maybe," Ez said.

Martha paused. "You think maybe Stevie ...?"

Ez did not answer.

Martha smiled a wry smile. She said gently, "You think it matter?"

Several expressions crossed Ez's face. Eventually he said, "You his mother. You don't think it matter?"

"I trust Stevie."

"Why you no worry?" Ez asked.

"Because," Martha said, "Stevie like you – full of loving-kindness. Everything you touch, you love. You love me, you love your son, you love this flat, you love your work." She halted. "What matter?"

Ez was silent for several seconds. After a while Martha said, "You even love de reptiles."

"I tink," Ez said, "maybe you exaggeratin'."

"Am I?"

Ez turned to her. "Woman, you got serpent tongue."

"I tink sometime, you like my serpent tongue, too."

They stared at each other. Ez said: "When you cookin' de fried lizard, woman?"

"Whyfor, man?"

"Celebration," Ez said. "I'm tinkin'."